and Venus among the fishes skips and is a she-dolphin
she is the gay, delighted porpoise sporting with love and the sea
she is the female tunny-fish, round and happy among the males
and dense with happy blood, dark rainbow bliss in the sea.

D. H. Lawrence, "Whales Weep Not!"

For David,
who has just discovered the world beneath the sea,
and to my dolphin swimming companions
Lil Bit, Dingy, Jessica, Sarah, and Samantha

FOREWORD

Scott O'Dell's last Christmas was spent at Hawk's Cay, Florida, where he was drawn to the dolphins who swam with hotel guests and performed in three shows daily. Each day he watched every show and often spoke of our first joint encounter with dolphins — in the glacial fjord called Lynn Canal, south of Skagway, Alaska, where in 1972 we picked up a pod of dolphins while cruising in our boat, *The Arctic Star*. The pod followed us for many miles, weaving a beautiful pattern as they surfed our bow wave. Later in the afternoon, just after we anchored in St. James Bay, they returned and slowly swam around the boat, so close that we could hear the sighs of their breathing. When we left Hawk's Cay, Scott put away the manuscript of *Thunder Rolling in the Mountains* and began to work on his dolphin story.

For five months, he worked on Coral's story. It went slowly, but he said that he was more excited about this book than any he had worked on for years. When his waning strength no longer would permit him to carry out the required research, he reluctantly laid aside the manuscript and returned to his Chief Joseph story, which placed fewer demands on his energy.

When I picked up the manuscript and began to flesh out the story, I discovered just how demanding the research was. Besides the voluminous reading, there were visits to marine labs and aquariums on the Atlantic and Pacific coasts, courses in marine ecology and in the biology and behavior of dolphins and whales, a visit to the navy training school for divers in Panama City, numerous snorkeling excursions, and periodic free swims with dolphins. I also dived into the sea to visit a submerged ambient-pressure habitat that, as La Chalupa, had once been situated one hundred feet under the surface, ten miles off the coast of Puerto Rico. This habitat is the model for the "sea-cave" in the story.

Coral and her companions communicate with clicks, whistles, and sound pictures, rather like sonograms. No one knows whether dolphins actually pass information through sound pictures, but they certainly project sound waves whose returning echoes give them a mental picture of their surroundings. If dolphins can reproduce the incoming echoes, they would have a way of letting other dolphins "see" what they have "seen."

In addition to works of marine biology and *Living*

and Working in the Sea by James Miller and Ian Koblick, the most helpful books were Karen Pryor's *Lads before the Wind,* Kenneth Norris's *Dolphin Days,* Pryor and Norris's *Dolphin Societies,* Sam Ridgway's *The Dolphin Doctor,* Richard O'Barry's *Behind the Dolphin Smile,* and Wade Doak's *Encounters with Whales and Dolphins.* They describe the amazing range of behavior shown by dolphins in captivity and in the wild. Especially valuable were discussions with Christopher Olstad, Operations Director for MarineLab Undersea Laboratory; my repeated opportunities to swim with a pod of five dolphins at Dolphins Plus in Key Largo; and the workshop conducted there by Russell McFee.

— Elizabeth Hall

VENUS

AMONG THE FISHES

1

It was just before dawn, when the sea was still black. I swam alone because it was my turn to keep close watch for killers.

Glacier Strait was peaceful before they came. Gentle sea tides ran in and out. Friendly mountains rose on both sides of us, covered with snow in the winter and sometimes in the summer. Small trees grew along the rocky shore, casting shadows on the water. Beneath the surface, fish searched for unwary crabs and jellyfish or scooped up krill, tiny creatures that drift with the tide. Near the rocks, sculpin hovered, hidden among the waving strands of seaweed. Below them, halibut and sole lay half buried in the sand.

As I watched, I swam in wide, slow circles in back of the dolphin herd. My farsensor swept the sea behind us, sending pulses of sound whose echoes would warn of approaching danger. I was searching for the herd of killer whales that had invaded our waters.

Dolphins filled Glacier Strait before these killer orcas came. Now there were only a few of us.

The killers came because the strait was full of salmon. At this season, the salmon were sluggish, heavy with eggs, and intent on reaching the streams where they were born. The salmon came each summer, but this was the first time they had been followed by killer whales. When the killers weren't eating salmon, they were eating dolphins.

As our herd shrank in size, it became dangerous to fish. Most of the older dolphins beat their fins against the water and whistled in despair, afraid that the killers would eat us all.

But my father did not give up. He was quick and clever, so clever that he had earned the name of Great Thinker. Father began posting a guard while we hunted and forbade any of us to stray from the herd, even if the rest of the pod went along. Since that time, the killers had caught only dolphins who wandered off by themselves.

My father was the largest male in our herd of white-sided dolphins. From his white face, a light stripe curved up over his head and along his gleaming black back to his white and black dorsal fin. His belly was a pearly white. Father was such a skillful swimmer that his skin had never been scraped or scarred, despite his many encounters with sharks, orcas, or angry dolphins.

As I watched for orcas now, my father and the older

males swam on the sides of the herd, looking for squid and herring. Our pod swam with other pods in the center, where it was safe.

I could hear the herd call as it moved through the water. Again and again each dolphin whistled its name and announced that all was well. The messages told the rest of the herd that it was safe to continue the hunt. At the first threatening echo from behind, I would stop whistling my name and warn the herd with the loud crack of sensor sound that signaled danger. Warnings travel fast beneath the water.

I had just scooped up a tender young rock sole when echoes from my farsensor gave a faint image of orcas moving toward us. The image soon became clear as the cry of a sea hawk. The killers were swimming fast.

I beamed an alarm. The warning rippled across the herd as dolphins passed on the cry, "Danger!" The pods huddled close together, making it hard for an orca to choose a target.

Father and the other large males moved to the rear of the herd and turned to face the oncoming orcas. Killers rarely attack a packed herd of dolphins, but sometimes they do strange things.

A dozen black fins cut through the water. Their leader was almost four times as long as my father and weighed nearly thirty times as much. His skin was glossy black, except for a large white patch behind each eye and a white throat and belly. Scattering a school of herring, he began to threaten us.

Like dolphins, orcas speak in whistles and squeals, squawks and creaks, clicks and barks. They can also roar, and that is just what the big orca did.

The roaring began while he was still five orca lengths away. He sent out a series of unpleasant sounds that came so rapidly they tumbled over one another. Although dolphins and orcas whistle different dialects, it was clear that he wanted us out of the strait. He seemed to feel that there was not enough fish to feed both orcas and dolphins. Mixed in with the warning was his name whistle, which sounded like "White Fang."

Orcas eat mostly salmon and trout — although their favorite food is a tender young seal pup. They will gobble up almost anything — fish, birds, dolphins, and even the biggest whales, if they get hungry enough. White Fang was telling us that his pod had big appetites.

This must be true, I thought, for he was enormous and the others who were gathered around him were almost as large. Their white bellies gleamed in the early dawn, and their massive bodies seemed to fill the strait.

White Fang's eyes flashed with anger, and he reared

high out of the water. His white throat and chest towered over my father.

My father played for time. He made friendly whistles that told the orca there was plenty of fish for everybody — as long as no one was greedy.

White Fang understood because he became even angrier. He thrashed his tail and sent a wave speeding across the strait. Then he roared again and showed his teeth.

Orcas have long, sharp teeth that curve wickedly in their great mouths. Those teeth are made for tearing, and they can snap off your head with a single bite or swallow you whole.

Father slowly repeated the friendly sounds.

At this, White Fang jerked his head and thrashed his tail again, splashing water in all directions. He plunged into our midst. We scattered.

I burst into the air. My blowhole whooshed open and I took a big breath, then dove beneath the killers. The water was murky, and nothing showed in the gloom. I clicked rapidly. The echoes revealed an enormous rock ahead and dolphins swimming in wide circles on the other side. I darted around the jagged edge of the rock and found the rest of our pod.

We turned to leave. The other pods fled. Before we could join them, my brother Snapper, who was still too young to swim with the males, did a foolish thing. He came up beneath White Fang, leaped high in the air, and bit a piece out of the killer's dorsal fin, the black fin that stands up on its back and looks like a sail.

White Fang plunged straight down. He was not gone long. He came up booming and spouting water. With an angry whistle, he called for the killers to attack.

In a battle we were no match for the killers. But instead of fleeing, Father swam straight at White Fang. The rest of our big males followed him.

This sudden assault surprised the big orca. He hesitated, and so did the rest of his pod.

"Go!" whistled Father.

The dolphin males made a sharp turn. Without another click or whistle, without even a tail slap, we left for the far end of the strait.

2

We swam steadily, leaping into the air to increase our speed. No one paused. Father and some of the other males crossed back and forth behind us, but the orcas did not follow.

At the far end of the strait, we caught up with the rest of the herd. Father signaled for the pods to follow. He led us into the bay, where we fished in the early morning light.

Before long, we found a large school of anchovies. The herd spread, surrounding the school. The frightened fish fled along the only path — toward land. They squeezed so closely together that they jostled one another. Pushed to the surface, their silver bodies glinted in the sun. The anchovies were caught between our herd and the shore. They could not escape.

When the pods had eaten their fill of fish, we swam to a shallow part of the bay, where orcas could not attack from below. There we took our daily rest.

The herd formed a circle. In the center were the babies and their mothers. Next to them were the young dolphins. The oldest and wisest dolphins stayed on the edges. We slept just below the surface of the sea, swimming in slow circles, with one eye open. If we slept soundly, we would forget to breathe, and we would drown.

The circle kept the younger dolphins from drifting out of their safe position. It also kept us in formation, ready to flee if some creature attacked.

On this morning, the attack came. Midway through our rest, White Fang and his killers burst through the water. They tried to push us against the shore, where we could not get away.

The shallow water served us well. Most of the herd slipped beneath the orcas, but our pod was trapped in a small inlet. There was no place for us to hide.

Just before the killers reached us, Snapper signaled. He whistled our names, "Mother! Coral! Urchin!" and sent an image of us swimming safely inside a rocky grotto. Snapper had found a narrow opening in the rocks that lined the shore.

We darted through the opening and found ourselves in a large cave. Between the water and the rock that arched above us was an air space. Safe for the moment, we watched the orcas swim around outside the entrance. Huddled against the cavern wall, my baby sister Urchin made small frightened noises.

Although Mother had said nothing and was quietly stroking Urchin, I could tell that she was ready to fight White Fang to protect her children.

On the other side of the narrow opening, the orcas slapped their tails in anger. Then everything grew quiet.

Through the cavern entrance, which was a mere slit in the rocks, I heard White Fang whistling to a young killer, barely a third his size. He ordered the youngster to swim through the passage.

There were squawks of protest, but after a roar from White Fang, the young orca obeyed. He pushed his head through the slit, but a flipper caught in the rocks and he couldn't budge. He twisted one way, then another, but he did not move the space of a seal's whisker.

Snapper whistled with excitement and charged toward the orca. It was clear that my brother intended to attack the trapped killer.

Before he could fasten his teeth in the orca's massive head, my mother signaled, "Back!" Inside the pod her word was law.

Snapper stopped so suddenly that he flipped over.

It was a good thing that he did, because while he was taking small bites out of the orca, the orca would have taken a big bite out of Snapper. Even though the orca was small, as orcas go, his teeth looked as if he could rip stone like seaweed.

We waited, scarcely daring to breathe. We could hear the other orcas splashing about and whistling to one another as they tried to free their companion. If they could not get him loose, he would drown.

That seemed like a good idea, but it did not please Mother. She rumbled unhappily and waved her flippers at the side of the cave. Each incoming swell reached a little higher than the one before it. The tide was coming in. Before long, the water would reach the roof of the cave. Then we wouldn't be able to breathe. With the killer's body blocking the entrance, we were trapped.

Mother thought a moment, then swam over to the struggling orca. She offered to help.

The young killer's eyes brightened, but she squawked at him several times before he understood that he was to keep his jaws closed.

He clamped his mouth tight and shut his eyes. Four of us shoved hard on his chin. On the other side of the opening, the orcas figured out what we were doing and pulled hard on his tail. We stretched him some, but after a while his head slipped back across the rocks. He pulled free, leaving smears of blood behind.

From outside came a flurry of whistles and growls and splashes. White Fang's mother scolded him for his foolishness and slapped him once with her flukes and twice with her flippers. He did not make a sound. Then his mother whistled words of comfort to the wounded orca.

With White Fang's mother in the lead, the killers swam away.

3

The killers did not bother us that night. Beneath a full moon, we played and leaped and fished until the sun rose.

With some of the other young dolphins, Snapper and I practiced spinning. One at a time, we dove below the others and signaled, "Spin!" Then we held ourselves upright and rocked back and forth. With several deep thrusts of our flukes, we burst high into the air, turning our bodies in a tight circle. As we fell back into the water, we slapped the surface loudly, then sank deeply into the sea, drawing a long trail of bubbles behind us. We had contests to see who could make the loudest smack as we reentered the water and who could produce the longest trail of bubbles.

Before we rested, Father swam over to our pod. He was worried. He feared that yesterday's attack in the bay meant we were in even greater danger.

All through the dark hours, the big males had muttered and moaned about the Great Orca Threat. Some hoped that the killers would leave our waters after the moon shrank and grew large again and the salmon stopped running. But deep within each big dolphin was the worry that the orcas would stay in Glacier Strait until they had eaten the last dolphin. We needed more large males. Many of the females were expecting young, and we had barely enough males to protect our small herd.

Father and Mother whistled softly. Mother was upset. While they talked, Father stroked her side. After a time, Mother sighed, sending a sad stream of bubbles to the surface. She had agreed to something she did not like.

Father signaled the rest of us to join them. With one eye on Mother and the other on me, he asked if I was brave enough to make a long journey — and to make it alone.

I had never thought of leaving the pod. I stared at him. My mouth opened wide, and my blowhole bubbled. Silence settled over the pod. You could hear scallops popping and salmon jumping far away in the strait.

Father sensed my surprise. Gradually, he made me understand that the big males had decided that I should go search for Silver, my older brother, who had left in search of adventure more than three summers ago.

Silver was a clever dolphin and almost as skillful as

Father. His intelligence and strength would increase the safety of all. Father put pictures in my head of Silver eluding White Fang and defending the young. Then he pictured the herd moving away from Glacier Strait, moving far south to a bay where sharks were few and orcas never came.

I understood that some of the big males wanted to leave the strait. On my journey, I was to search for safer waters. If I could not find Silver, the herd would move.

What I did not understand was why the herd did not move now. Before I could return with Silver, the orcas might kill many more dolphins.

Father glanced around the pod, from one of us to the other. His eye was dull. He told us that too many of the females were expecting a child. Until the births were over, they would find the long trip too difficult. Birthing dolphins in strange waters made females so uneasy that they had a difficult time and sometimes lost their babies.

The thought of traveling far from my pod upset me. I would be alone. Never in my life had I been without the company of other dolphins.

Mother sensed my concern. She was always quick to understand our feelings. She whistled Snapper's name, then mine. She did this three times.

I understood that Snapper was to go with me. He

was almost large enough to leave the pod, but not large enough to defend us against orcas. His departure would not weaken the herd.

Snapper understood her, too. He became so excited that all the sounds he sent winging out sounded like one. He rose up in the water, all but his tail, and stroked backward. When he was a dolphin length away, he leaped high in the air and spun around twice before he fell back with a loud splash.

Snapper made so much noise that he woke Urchin, who was drifting drowsily in the shelter of my flipper. She tossed her tail, swam over to Mother, and snuggled against her.

Father was not pleased with Snapper's playfulness. He buzzed a warning and clapped his jaws. Then he let us know about the dangers that lay in strange waters. We might encounter orcas. We might encounter hungry sharks. Even worse, we might encounter humans.

I didn't understand the signal for humans. I squawked twice to let Father know that the signal was strange to me.

He told me they were the creatures who lived inside the boats we sometimes saw in the distance, the boats that took fish from the sea. Then he put surprising pictures in my head. I saw creatures with long, bony tentacles and no fins. Their skin was dry, and something like strands of living fishnet grew out of their heads. On their flukes, they moved about in dry air and peered over the side of their boats. Then I saw them throwing nets over dolphins and pulling them out of the water. A shiver as cold as an iceberg went down my spine.

Father swam around Snapper and me in tight circles, looking closely at us with each pass. He was waiting for my answer.

Mother whistled softly and stroked me with her flippers.

I struggled to make up my mind. The struggle had nothing to do with the help Mother would need when the new baby arrived. It had nothing to do with Urchin's care. It had only a little to do with the loneliness that I would feel when I left the herd. I hesitated because I was terrified at the thought of these strange humans.

Father waited. The minutes dragged by. Three times I surfaced to breathe without answering.

At last I replied. Pushing down my fears, I signaled "Yes." I would make the journey.

4

On the morning we left Glacier Strait, a heavy fog hid the sun. The fog was so thick that when we surfaced to breathe we saw only a swirling, white mist.

It was not a long farewell. I told Urchin to be sure and stay close to Mother when they were out fishing and always to watch for White Fang and his herd. To keep up my own courage, I told my mother that I would be back soon to help with the new baby.

Mother said that I should not worry about her. She and Urchin would swim with her sister's pod and would not be lonely. It hadn't occurred to me that she would be lonely, but I was careful not to say so.

Father said I should watch out for strange dolphins. Roving groups of young males sometimes surrounded females who were separated from their own pod, hoping to steal a mate for one of the gang.

This was one danger that did not frighten me. I bobbed my head impatiently. I could take care of myself. I sent Father a sound picture to remind him that

I swam faster than any of the young males in our herd.

Father was still concerned about our safety. Again he told us to watch out for orcas. He pictured White Fang lurking where the strait met the bay, waiting for stray dolphins.

I decided Father was feeling guilty about sending us off alone. The orcas were resting. They always dozed when the morning was heavy with fog. By the time it burned off, we'd be on our way.

We were ready to go, but Father was not finished. His final warning was the most ominous. He filled our heads with pictures of humans killing dolphins and seals and ordered us to flee if a boat came near. In his long life, Father had seen humans kill every creature in the sea. They were worse than orcas, he whistled, because they were the only creatures who made killing a game.

Sobered by his last warning, I swam off in the lead. I maintained a lively pace, but Snapper was so excited he leaped and splashed, making wide circles around me.

He made such a commotion that I feared he would wake the sleeping orcas. With a series of short clicks, I told him to stop his nonsense and keep watch for the killers. If he didn't, I would send him home.

Obediently, Snapper fell beside me. Every few minutes he scanned behind us and signaled that the killers were not within sensor range. But at midmorning, when the fog had vanished and we glided happily along in the sun, he clicked a warning. Through the water came the echo pattern produced by a killer whale. By copying the pattern, Snapper warned me without alerting the orcas.

I glanced back. There in the middle of the strait and close I saw ten tall fins cutting the water. A stout wind was blowing, and the tall fins looked like sails. The killers looked like ten sailboats sailing toward us.

Without wasting a second, I led Snapper to the bottom of the strait. We picked up speed, and when we came to the surface for air, the killers had not gained on us. We went down again and swam along the murky bottom, rising only to grab quick breaths. Even Snapper swam steadily and wasted no time in play. When the sun was overhead the orcas were still far behind us.

The strait narrowed, and the water changed its color, from blue to a glittering red. It was choked with salmon eager to lay their eggs in their home stream. The thought of a salmon sliding down my throat made me hungry, but if we slowed to eat the orcas would be upon us. We swam on, hoping that the orcas would linger.

There were so many salmon in this part of the strait

that we had to stay close to the bank and keep a sharp watch for rocks and sunken logs. It took us until mid-afternoon to reach the end of the strait.

Here a big river flowed into Wolf Bay. On the far side of the bay the sea began. We got to the river just as the tide came rushing in from the sea. The two crashed into each other with a roar.

Waves swept the bay. Hills of water reared up, toppled, and reared up again. As the water was sucked away, the rocky bottom showed. The water tumbled violently in one direction, then in the other, then in all directions at once. Yellow mist filled the sky.

Snapper clapped his flippers. He was set to dive into the midst of the battle.

The swirling waters looked dangerous. Echoes from them showed broken pieces of timber and hunks of metal strewn across the bottom. The forces were strong enough to tear apart ships. If they pulled us down and tumbled us about, we could drown.

I ordered Snapper to stay beside me. We would wait until the tide turned and ran back to the sea and the bay was calm.

Snapper protested, but he followed me to a place at the riverbank hidden by willow trees. We had scarcely settled ourselves behind the screen of trailing branches when White Fang and his killers swam by.

They didn't see us. They didn't stop. They sailed

into the battle. One after the other, ten of them, with their tall fins sticking straight up. Through the mist I caught glimpses of them as the waves tossed them about. But their powerful tails drove them on toward the far shore.

The river gave up the battle. It broke into two streams. One ran off to the right, hugging the shore. The other stream ran to the left. We took the left stream and soon came to the opening where the sea began. There were high mountains on both sides of us, and we swam with the tide until we came to the open sea and a small island.

At once, at the far end of the island, we detected White Fang and his group. Soon afterward we heard them whistling.

At any moment they might detect us. I thought hard. Over short distances we could outrun the orcas. Our only chance was to move out fast.

My farsensor picked up a strange object. The echoes were loud and clear. It was a ship.

The ship moved slowly. Now we heard the creaking and rumbling and swishing sounds it made. It was coming closer.

My first stomach churned with fear. A ship meant humans, and humans meant danger. Perhaps we should simply hide and hope that the shelter of the island would keep White Fang from sensing us.

Snapper felt no such fear. Before I could signal him, he swam away. Intent on the rushing waves made by the ship's progress, he leaped out of the water in front of the ship. Whistling with joy, he began riding the bow wave.

Creatures that must have been humans leaned over the ship's side. Each time Snapper leaped into the air, they made loud noises and gestured with their tentacles. Snapper circled the ship three times, but the humans did not harm him.

The ship moved steadily toward White Fang and his herd, who were twittering about what a fine dinner a few dolphins would make. The noise of engines rumbled through the water, but the orcas were so busy plotting that they didn't notice. I don't believe they sensed the ship, not until the very moment that the net sailed out and settled around White Fang.

The twittering stopped. Quickly, they gathered in a circle. With all of them talking at once, they tried to decide how best to get him loose.

White Fang twisted to one side and the other. He dove, but his tail got tangled in the net. He turned on his back and beat the water with his powerful flippers. He showed his dozens of teeth and slashed at the net. Through it all, his raspy voice rose and fell, gently pled for help, boomed out terrible threats. His pod swam helplessly in circles, still not knowing what to do.

Snapper was so excited by the orca's capture that he swam over for a close look. This was a foolish thing to do, and I sent sound pictures of a net dropping over his own body.

Snapper took this picture of danger as a challenge to be brave. He began to swim back and forth beside the net, moving closer with each pass. He swam so close that he could brush White Fang's head with his flippers.

The net began to rise in the water. To his surprise, Snapper rose with it.

Desperate, I swam to his side, making no attempt to hide my presence. As the net neared the surface, I pulled down one edge so that Snapper could swim out.

We watched as the net broke the water and hung above the surface, with White Fang tangled helplessly in the mesh. I thought that the people on the ship would use their tentacles like an octopus, wrapping them around White Fang and pulling him onto the deck. But they did not touch him. As the heavy weight rose, the ship tilted and green water swept over the deck.

Quickly, the net steadied, swung lower, and hauled

the orca over the side. With a great splash, White Fang dropped into a tank of water. He was almost as big as the tank.

The ship's sounds grew loud, and it moved away fast. The herd of killers swam after it, leaping high out of the water, making wild sounds of sorrow. Their interest in dolphins had vanished.

I felt a surge of joy. Perhaps the orcas would follow the boat far into the south and never return to Glacier Strait. If they did not come back, our journey would be over and we could go home.

We decided to stay near the island until we were certain. Snapper promised that he would not go near another boat.

5

All night we waited in a sheltered cove. At dusk the next day, the orcas returned. Worn out by the chase, they swam past us on their way home. White Fang's mother led them, making sad, mournful whistles as she moved slowly through the water.

By sunrise the orcas would be back in Glacier Strait. We could not go home. Sadly, we left the island behind us and headed south. There was a mountain shore on our left side, and on the right side were low-lying islands. For five days we traveled between them in calm water.

On the fifth day at dusk the last of the islands disappeared and we were in open water. The shore lay on our left, and on our right the sea stretched as far as we could see. The ocean looked different here. Far behind us, where it met the sky, a gray hill rose up. It was a hill of water, a great smooth swell. Behind it was another, and behind that another. These swells rolled on, one after the other, and never stopped.

Snapper made a game around the swells. He glided

on the surface of each one, rising up, then sliding down the long slope on the other side.

I was accustomed to the calm waters of Glacier Strait, but I soon discovered that the heaving water at our backs was helping us along our way. We were in a slow, silent river that carried us south.

Each day we traveled farther from our home. Each night the moon above the vast ocean grew smaller. Now it was no more than a sliver in the night sky, yet we found no trace of my brother. I had no idea where to look for him. I wondered if we would ever find him. Sometimes I thought that Father and Mother had sent us away to save us from the orcas' slashing teeth.

On the twelfth day, with the sun high overhead, I heard a ponderous rumble behind me. It sounded as if a big ship was about to overtake us. I turned to sense the object and saw the head of a great beast rise out of the sea. Startled, I moved close to Snapper.

The beast seemed peaceful. As I looked at it more closely, I decided it must be a whale. Nothing else could be that big.

I had heard about whales from my father, who had seen them once in Big Bay. But nothing that he said made it possible for me to believe my eyes. This one was so large that it made White Fang seem like a baby.

The whale opened its jaws as it came upon us. I

could have swum through them without touching the sides. Both of us could have swum through them without touching the sides.

Luckily, there were no teeth in that gaping mouth. Instead, stiff, overlapping plates lined the vast opening. The plates ended in a row of long, coarse bristles. Behind the plates, I saw a tongue as big as an entire pod of dolphins.

With its mouth stretched wide, the whale dived. In a few minutes it came up with a mouthful of water. From the closed jaws, water streamed through the bristle curtain that captured small fish and krill. Behind the whale rose a cloud of mud.

The great mouth opened again. The whale still seemed peaceful.

The whale had blotchy gray skin. She had no fins on her back, but there was a row of bumps along her spine. She spouted a shining, heart-shaped cloud.

Her clicks and whistles were a rumble and roar that seemed to come from the bottom of the sea. She wanted to know where we were going.

I tried whistling, but she did not understand me. Then I tried sending sound pictures. I pictured our brother swimming away and us searching for him, but she looked blank. But when I pictured the orca herd attacking dolphins, she understood at once.

She groaned an enormous groan, a groan that was

full of pain. The sound drowned out the cry of gulls flying overhead.

Suddenly, sound pictures formed in my head. I saw the whale give birth to a fine calf with smooth gray skin and a lovely arch to his mouth. There was not a scar or a barnacle on his body. I saw the whale caring for her calf, nursing it, and playing with it.

I glanced at Snapper. For once, he was still, intent on the sound pictures sent by the whale.

The pictures changed. I saw the young whale splashing about and showing his mother how deep he could dive. I watched as the pair were separated and the young whale surfaced in a pod of orcas. He was too young to be afraid. Before the whale could reach him, an orca grabbed his flippers and tossed him onto his back. As the pack moved in to feed, the water turned red.

The whale stopped sending pictures and sighed. Her great body shuddered. I could feel her sorrow.

For a while we swam in silence. As I thought about the orcas, I became angry. I was glad that the humans had captured White Fang. I wished that they had captured the entire pod of orcas. Then Snapper and I could go home. I thought so hard that I didn't notice the blue sky and the wispy clouds, the warm winds and the gentle current. I didn't notice them until

Snapper leaped high and splashed down almost on top of me.

I clapped my jaws in anger, and Snapper backed off. He stopped frolicking and swam by my side, matching me stroke for stroke.

The whale seemed amused by Snapper. With a gesture of her flippers, she invited him to ride her pressure wave.

I could scarcely believe her offer. With us riding her wave, she would have to stay near the surface. The offer seemed kind, but perhaps she was trying to lure us close. Perhaps she swallowed dolphins whole. As Snapper got ready to dart into her wave, I pulled him back.

The whale was surprised. Once again, she beckoned with a flipper.

This time Snapper was too quick for me. He moved in close to her side and began to enjoy the free ride.

I hesitated. I matched the whale's speed but kept my distance. While Snapper surfed, I stroked steadily with my flukes, hurrying to keep up. We traveled this way for a long time. The water sparkled green and clear.

As the sun moved down toward the sea, I decided that the whale meant no harm. Taking a deep breath, I slipped in beside Snapper and relaxed. The water rushed along my sides, its foamy bubbles tickling my skin.

The trip was so pleasant that I almost forgot to scan regularly for dolphins. Even if we did not meet Silver, we might encounter a dolphin who could give us news of him. From time to time, I sent out sensor pulses, but detected nothing except fish, seals, and once, when the water grew shallow, an angel shark hidden in the sand, hoping for a careless halibut.

Suddenly, a series of pictures formed in my head. I saw a ship appear at our side. Then I saw the whale dive, so deep the light was gone and the world was black.

The whale was trying to tell me something. I signaled that I did not understand.

Again the pictures formed. This time, they were followed by more pictures. I saw humans throwing long metal bars. The bars stuck into the whale's body. Blood covered the sea, and the whale died.

The message finally became clear. At dawn, humans had chased the whale. They tried to kill her, but she escaped by diving to the bottom. She had not seen them all day, but feared that they were still after her. If their ship appeared, she would dive deep and leave us behind.

I felt sad. The whale had lost her child to orcas and might lose her life to humans. Yet she had befriended us, who were so small in her eyes. I thought about her troubles and about ours. Despite our difference in size, we had common enemies.

No ships appeared. The sun slipped into the sea, and the sky turned red. We sailed along with the whale's huge tail moving steadily up and down. Waves rolled in, but not once did we come close to being washed away from her side. For the time being, we felt safe.

6

~~~~~~

Our happiness did not last long. At dawn we rounded a rocky headland. The sea was calm, but close in front of us spread what looked like a sheet of ice. The whale stopped. I had been coasting along on her tail wave, and the stop was so sudden that I smacked into her pectoral fin.

For a long time, she floated in silence beside the shining surface. Then she signaled that she did not understand what lay before us.

I was as baffled as the whale.

Far sensing didn't help. We detected a line of floating objects, but whatever it was that covered the sea sent back no echoes.

Snapper dipped a flipper into the shimmering surface. He squealed a warning. The shine was not ice. It was not oil. It was a net with meshes as thin as a krill's antenna. Yet no ship was in sight.

The net touched the shore and stretched far out in front of us. I dove straight down, keeping my flippers away from the mesh. The net extended far, far beneath the surface. It disappeared into the darkness.

Warily, we began to swim around the net. It was filled with salmon, with shark, with swordfish, with fish of every kind. Schools of squid were entangled. Birds hung lifeless, their feathers soggy. A great sea turtle drifted beside the net, the mesh wound round its limbs. There was a strange creature caught in the net. It lay on its back, its eyes staring, and fibers like seaweed streamed from its head. It must have been one of the humans Father had warned me about. I counted three sea lions and more dolphins than I had numbers for. All of them were dead except one dolphin, who had been caught at the surface and was able to breathe.

Angry pictures formed in my head. The whale thought that humans had set the net and that it had drifted from far away, on the other side of the ocean. The pictures she sent made me angry, too. Father was right. Humans killed everything that swam in the ocean.

I swam over and whistled to the dolphin. She looked up at me but did not answer. Her eyes were dull, as if she had given up all hope of rescue.

I had never seen a dolphin like her. Her back was a dark gray that became lighter on her sides, and her belly was white, like ours. She had a long, narrow black beak, just the color of her flippers, and a black ring surrounded each eye. Her flippers were long and tapered to a point. She was so thin I could almost see through her.

The dolphin lay still, without moving so much as the tip of a flipper. But I sent the "lie still" signal anyway, fearing that if she thrashed about, she would become hopelessly entangled.

She seemed to understand me.

Snapper and I looked at each other. The whale could not help us. We would have to free the dolphin by ourselves.

Taking care not to get caught in the wall of death, we took hold of the net with our teeth. It was made of strands so thin that we could scarcely see them. We worked at the mesh and carefully slipped it off. It was slow work, even though the dolphin was caught by only one flipper.

When at last she was free, she did not try to swim, but lay motionless. Snapper and I slipped under her flippers and held her up to keep her from sinking.

I asked her if she would like to come with us. She tried to answer, but she was too weak to whistle or click. She wobbled and rolled her eyes.

I was afraid to leave her. If we swam away, she might wander back into the net and starve to death — if she didn't drown first. But she was too weak to stay afloat, even in the whale's bow wave.

We looked helplessly at one another. I don't know what we would have done if the whale had not had an idea. She pictured the dolphin moving just below the surface while lying still. She was resting on the whale's broad back. Each time the whale came up for air, the dolphin breathed. It seemed worth a try.

We had a hard time getting the new dolphin onto the whale's back. She was slippery from all the algae she had gathered. She kept sliding off one side, then the other.

A whistle of protest escaped my blowhole. Even if we could get the dolphin into position, she would slide into the sea each time we encountered a swell. I was ready to give up.

Then the whale had another idea. She sent new pictures. This time all of us were riding on her back.

She slipped under the surface and waited. Snapper got on one side of the new dolphin, and I got on the other.

We nudged the dolphin into position between us, but moved her with great care. Along the whale's back, from neck to tail, grew patches of barnacles, each one sharper than a shark's tooth. Some of the patches were white, and some were orange. Any one of them could give us a nasty scratch.

The whale swam off slowly, with deliberate strokes

of her tail, warily watching the net. We swam for hours. As the sun set, we came to the end of it.

We rounded the end of the net and turned back toward the coast, swimming along the path the moon was making on the sea. The black-beaked dolphin seemed stronger. The gasping had stopped, and she breathed steadily. She was going to recover.

If we were going to swim together, we would have to know the new dolphin's name signal. Now that she was breathing easily, she might be able to tell us. I whistled my name and then the signal that meant a question. I whistled three times before she answered me.

The dolphin's whistle was so soft I could hardly understand. At last I caught her meaning. Her whistle was "Sea Fan," which was a beautiful sound.

I signaled Snapper that Sea Fan was a perfect signal for such a strange but lovely creature. He made protesting noises and sent a picture of her head, with its long, black beak. He thought that beautiful dolphins had pleasing blunt beaks like ours.

The sun was high before we neared the coast. The morning was calm. The sea glittered. A gentle breeze blew in from the hills, and there wasn't a cloud in the sky.

Sea Fan grew strong enough to stay on the whale's back without help. As soon as she signaled us, Snapper leaped into the sea and played games with the whale's huge tail that went slowly up and down, up and down. He darted around it. He dodged in and out of the sparkling waves it made. He let it toss him high in the air. He hung onto the tail and went up and down.

I watched until I could resist no more. Then I slipped off the whale's back and joined Snapper. The new dolphin watched us and seemed to enjoy our antics.

We frolicked until the sun was overhead and the whale stopped to rest. That afternoon we swam steadily until we ran into a school of sardines. We had not eaten for a long time. At home, we would have surrounded the school, driving them together in the center. But there were too few of us.

The whale tried to help us. She slapped her tail hard on the water and blasted with her sensor. The double impact stunned the fish, and they were too dazed to dart away.

To be courteous we waited for the whale to eat first. She took half the school in one swallow, and the rest of the school in the next swallow. As the water trailed out through her bristles, she signaled that she preferred the krill she scooped from the bottom.

Strays scooted off, and Snapper swam after them. One at a time, he brought them back for the new dolphin.

The next time we ran into a school, we did not wait for the whale. We blasted the fish with far sensing sound, then drove the stunned school toward the shore.

Near land, the water swarmed with fish. They leaped into the air and fell back again. Before we could take a mouthful, gulls came from every direction. Their fluttering wings and frenzied screams filled the sky. The birds dived into the middle of the school, snatching fish in the air, from the water, and from the mouths of other gulls. We paid no attention to them. The school was so big that there was plenty for all.

We were still eating sardines when a deep, rhythmic thrashing echoed through the water. Without a word, the whale left us. Her flukes broke the water, and she dove deep, far into the black depths below. The only sign of her presence was a large, flat ring of water where she had been swimming. Then, close to us, I saw a gray ship sailing along the shore.

We went on eating. The ship circled the place where the whale had gone down. It made three slow circles. The humans on its deck paid no attention to us. Then the ship drifted down the shore and disappeared.

Sea Fan wondered where the whale had gone.

Snapper answered her by repeating the whale's sound picture of humans killing a whale.

Sea Fan understood. She squealed in fear, then tried to push the pictures out of our heads. She had seen humans kill whales in the southern seas, and the sight was so horrible she could not stand to think about it.

Snapper sent more pictures. He thought that the whale had recognized the ship. She was in danger, and she knew it. She was hiding. He feared we would never see our friend again.

My farsensor told me he was right. The whale was moving swiftly out to sea along the ocean floor. Her echoes grew fainter and fainter.

We wondered what we would do without our huge, gentle friend. Sea Fan was still weak. There was no way we could carry her on our backs.

For the rest of the afternoon, we drifted, waiting for Sea Fan to grow stronger. When she signaled that she was ready, we started south. As we moved slowly through the water, the last rays of the sun reddened the evening sky.

7

We didn't see the gray ship again or any sign of the whale. We traveled slowly through the night beneath a cloudy sky. Sometimes we swam. Sometimes, when the new dolphin got weary, we floated. We didn't go far.

At sunrise the water was filled with the rhythmic swish and rumble of the gray ship. Far beyond us, where the sky met the sea, I saw its small dark shape. I dove and turned on my farsensor. The ship was sailing around in wide circles. The whale was in the center of the circles, swimming far down and fast.

"Trouble! Trouble!" I signaled. "Our friend in trouble." I could think of nothing to do.

Sea Fan whistled fearfully. She sent awful pictures of humans killing the whale, then turning on us. Humans could kill dolphins as easily as they killed whales.

As usual, Snapper didn't think. He acted. He started swimming toward the ship, as fast as he could move his tail.

Sea Fan and I looked at each other. We couldn't let him go into danger by himself. We swam after him.

In a few minutes we caught up with him. I moved alongside so that I could look into his eye.

"Slow!" I signaled. "Slow down!" I sent warnings of danger ahead.

Snapper paid no attention.

Sea Fan pictured an ocean full of whales. She suggested that the whale beneath the ship might be a stranger.

Snapper snorted, his blowhole opening and closing. He pictured our friend spouting, as she always did — two little spouts, then a big one.

As the picture filled our heads, the whale came up to breathe. Two little spouts and a big heart-shaped one rose between us and the ship. It was our friend. She was between a thick kelp bed and the ship.

We argued about what to do. Secretly, I hoped that the whale would swim far away before she surfaced. Then she might escape on her own.

A small boat appeared from behind the large gray ship. Three humans were perched on it.

Sea Fan signaled that this boat did the killing. She had seen such boats in the southern seas. She showed us a big metal bar coming from the boat and striking the whale.

Snapper wanted to swim fast and smash a hole in the boat. Then it would sink and leave the humans floundering in the water.

I stared at Snapper with my right eye. I sent a picture of him with a broken beak. When that didn't change his mind, I pictured him sinking into the sea, his blood staining the green water.

Snapper paid no attention. He puffed out his sides with air. He swam very fast and struck the middle of the boat a hard blow. The boat rocked. The men rocked. But no harm was done except to Snapper, who was stunned. He rolled over on his back, his pale belly barely moving. If he took a breath, he would drown. I rushed in, flipped him over, and dragged him away.

The humans paid no attention to us. Their eyes were on the whale. She had finished breathing. She was diving. Only her tail showed in the air. The boat coughed blue smoke, and the humans headed for the place where she had gone down.

I followed her with my farsensor. She was swimming very fast along the edge of the kelp bed. The boat changed its course, circled around her, and stopped in a patch of sunshine where the kelp met the open sea. The humans had decided that this was where she would have to breathe again.

The whale was cornered. The three of us swam rapidly in her direction.

When we came upon her, she was only a short distance from the open sea. She was swimming far below us, down deeper than we dared to go. We sent out showers of warning clicks, the loudest warning we could send. She didn't answer them. She may have been so frightened that she didn't hear us.

She came up near the humans in the killer boat. I don't believe that she saw them. The two small spouts went up, then the tall one. Rainbows danced in the mist.

Our friend took in air for a long time. Two whale lengths away, a human crouched in the bow of the boat.

I still believe that she didn't see it. I warned her again. This warning she heard. With a swish of her mighty tail she started straight down.

The boat was rocking in the rough waves. The humans staggered. But they did not stop. There was a loud clap like thunder, and a metal bar whizzed through the air. It missed her and fell into the sea. Another clap and a second bar struck near her tail just as she disappeared. It had a rope tied to the end, and as she went down into deep water, the rope stiffened and the boat leaped forward.

The whale was caught. Now she had to pull the heavy boat. And when she came up to breathe again, the humans would know exactly where she was. They would be waiting.

The only way to save her was to cut the rope.

Without a click or a whistle, without sending a single sound picture, the three of us dived. We followed the rope down as far as we dared go. Dolphins have lots of teeth. They're small but very sharp. Again and again, we bit at the rope. We had frayed it almost in two when a dull thud from below sent us tumbling. The sea shuddered.

Sea Fan whistled in terror. She pictured exploding metal slicing through the whale's body.

The rope curved away over our heads. The whale was still alive. She was coming up to breathe. She broke the surface, took a deep breath, and went down again. Blood streamed from her tail and covered the slick patch of water.

The rope stiffened again, and we used our teeth, working frantically to free her. Only a few strands were left when the whale came up again. This time the boat was close by. I told her that we would soon have the rope broken in two.

The humans heard the loud whistles and peered around to find out where the sounds came from. Then one of them stood up and pointed a long stick at us.

There was a sharp crack. Bits of hot metal coursed through the water, and one glanced off my back. The pain made me wince. Blood streamed down my side. The pieces of metal glanced everywhere.

Before we could flee, before the whale could suck in the air she needed, another metal bar flew out from the boat. It sank deep and brought forth a fountain of blood.

She tried to dive, but she fell over and floated on her back. We watched while the humans sailed up beside her. One human leaned over the side and stuck a long pole into her belly. A small piece of cloth flapped at the end of the pole. Then they cut her loose. As they started off, the big gray ship moved toward the dead whale. We watched until the humans tied her to the ship and some of them crawled on her back and began to cut her up into pieces.

I turned away. I could watch no longer. None of us could. Our friend was gone.

The day was fading fast. Black clouds swept in from the land. As we swam beneath the racing clouds, my heart was full of sorrow for the whale and hatred for the humans who killed her.

8

The next night we traveled beneath clouds of sparkling stars. At dawn, waves beat against high stone cliffs, and far beyond the sun shone on a mountain peak covered with snow. It made me think of the snowy peaks in Glacier Strait and the sea tides that ran there and the home I had left. It made me sad to think of them. It made me sad to think of the whale, too.

Sea Fan saw that I was sad. She stroked my side with her flipper and whistled softly. She wondered if my back still hurt.

The problem was not my wound. My back was healed. At first it bled steadily. Then blubber oozed into the wound and closed it. Soon only a white scar would remind me of our encounter with the whale killers.

I whistled the whale's signal and groaned to let Sea Fan know how much I missed our friend.

Sea Fan answered with a sad whistle. She pictured the whale carrying us on her back and helping us find fish. Then she pictured a mother dolphin caring for her young. She was telling me that the whale was like a mother to us.

Even Snapper was sad. He had swum for hours without playing a trick or trying to start a game. All at once, he perked up. With a shout, he sped away.

A short distance ahead swam a school of anchovies. We hurried toward them in the hope of filling our stomachs.

Before we reached the school, it exploded. Through its center plunged the black bodies of cormorants, their wings tight at their sides, legs kicking. Their beaks snapped wickedly. The anchovies scattered, their bodies streaks of silver as they darted from danger. Frightened fish smacked against my head and pelted my sides. The unlucky were snatched up by the birds. The rest regrouped some distance behind us. We swam on, unwilling to retrace our path.

We had not gone far before we came upon an enormous kelp forest. It reached from the shore all the way to the islands that lay on the western horizon.

We had traveled along the fringes of other kelp forests, but had never entered them. This time we had no choice. If we kept to the edges we would have to swim far into the vast ocean, adding another day to our journey.

The trees in this forest stretched forever — from

the rocks on the bottom to the air above the sea. On the surface, a tangled canopy of brown kelp fronds moved back and forth in the currents and waves. Kelp-fish, exactly the color of seaweed, swayed in the same rhythm.

Below the canopy, the towering trunks were so close together that we swam in single file. Sunlight streamed through the pale water, casting a golden glow on the leafy fronds below. Moon jellies drifted among the swaying kelp trees, and spider crabs scuttled along the branches. Pink snails grazed near them. As we swam deeper, we saw fish everywhere. Fish cruised in the spaces between the kelp trees and hovered among the branches.

The kelp forest was a noisy place. Some fish squeaked, others grunted. Crabs popped like break-ing bubbles. Shrimp snapped. Clams and scallops clicked.

The morning was half gone when we came to an opening in the forest. It made a small lagoon, where glossy brown otters drifted on their backs. Some slept, their paws crossed on their chests, their flipperlike feet extended stiffly before them. Strands of kelp wrapped around their bodies kept them from drifting away.

The first otter we came upon was so busy he didn't see us. He lay upon his back. A flat stone rested on his belly. Grasped in his paws was a spiky, purple sea urchin. He struck it against the stone.

The otter kept beating the urchin against the stone and paid no attention to us. When the shell cracked open, he looked up and opened his mouth. Every tooth was purple. He fixed his large eyes on me and wiggled his whiskers. Then he scooped out the meat, thrust it at me, and made funny chirping sounds.

I took the meat in my mouth. It was the color of a halibut's belly but sweet. I flipped it around and swallowed it. It was delicious, but not the food for me. My flippers could never break open an urchin's shell.

The otter had no trouble. In a few minutes, he had freed the meat from another urchin. He threw his head back and lifted the urchin to his mouth. With a few bites of his sharp teeth, it was gone.

Dozens of otters were gathered in the lagoon. Some pounded clams or abalones or crabs with stones. Others dived or rolled about in the water, swimming backward at great speed. Their frolics did not seem to disturb the sleepers.

Our friend wrapped himself in one of the kelp strands and was closing his eyes when I heard a sound behind us. It was only a whisper, like a spring wind in trees along the riverbank.

Two humans were coming toward us in a small boat. One was paddling, and the other held a stick like the whale killer's stick that spit hot metal. There was a sharp explosion, and the otters dove out of sight.

We dove, too. We swam underwater until we had left the humans far behind.

A nagging worry that had been buried for several days came back. The humans seemed to be everywhere. I wondered if the humans had killed Silver — or if they would kill us before we found him.

We kept close to the shore in the hope of finding our brother. Each time we passed a bay or inlet, we swam into it, looking for him. As we swam through its waters, we whistled his name again and again. Always I feared that our whistles would be heard by humans, for the shore was the place where they gathered.

Sea Fan, who had nearly died in the humans' drift net, was as frightened of humans as I was. Whenever we swam near a shore where boats clustered, she made small, unhappy noises.

Once when she did this, I signaled her, asking if all was well.

She turned her head away so that I no longer could see her eye. We swam for several minutes in silence. "Afraid," she signaled at last. "Humans."

I let her know that I was afraid of humans, too.

Sea Fan moved close to me, so close that our flippers touched. We breathed in unison, rising to the surface for air without breaking contact. Sharing our fears made us feel closer, but the worry did not go away.

At last the forest narrowed, and we decided to leave it for the sea. Sounding only the path ahead, we moved into open water. The mistake was almost fatal.

We had traveled a short distance when Sea Fan, who now was swimming several flipper lengths to my right, whistled, turned abruptly, and crashed into me. Echoes brought back the pattern of sharks — six of them.

Until Sea Fan whistled, I believe that the sharks had not seen us. They had been hovering just outside the kelp forest, waiting for careless swimmers. And we were careless.

Alerted by the whistle, the sharks moved rapidly through the water. They were five dolphin lengths behind us and closing fast. In a few seconds they would reach us.

My first impulse was to swim off, as fast as I could. I headed for the surface. In my terror, I had forgotten the first safety rule of the sea. But Sea Fan remembered.

"School!" she screamed.

I turned abruptly. The three of us closed ranks, swimming in formation, our bodies nearly touching. Together, we darted back toward the forest, all moving at the same speed and matching our movements.

The sharks drew nearer. They were almost upon us. They were so close I could see their eyes, big as sand dollars. Their sharp teeth glistened.

We swerved right, then left. The sharks lunged at us. I heard the click as their jaws snapped shut. Their teeth closed on water.

We escaped into the kelp. If Sea Fan had not kept her head, at least one of us would now be shark dinner. For some reason, sharks are confused when dolphins stay in a tight school. They find it hard to focus on one dolphin when we all move together.

As we moved south through the forest, I realized that humans were not the only danger we faced.

9

The day dawned bright and cloudless. We swam near the shore, below high cliffs. At their base, waves crashed against black rocks in a shower of spray. It was a happy morning. The water gleamed green in the sunlight. Our stomachs were full of fish.

Snapper found a piece of seaweed trailing in the water and made up a new game. He draped the seaweed over a flipper and swam near me. Then he tossed it into the air and circled nearby.

I caught the seaweed with my beak and swam away fast, followed by Snapper. We tossed it back and forth several times, then I carried it to Sea Fan and shook it in her face.

Her eyes brightened, and she dove beneath me, coming up on the other side. She whistled, and I flipped the seaweed to her. With a flick of her tail, she pitched it onto her flipper and dragged it in front of Snapper. Just as he lunged for it, she tossed it to me. Together we played Keep-away, while Snapper darted back and forth, trying to grab the flying seaweed. It was the first time Sea Fan had shown interest in play-ing.

When we tired of the game, I let Snapper grab the end of the seaweed in his teeth. He pulled, but to his surprise, I did not let go. Snapper tugged again, harder this time. The seaweed stretched, then broke with a jerk, throwing Snapper backward. Sea Fan and I whistled with glee and swam off together.

As Sea Fan swam steadily through the bright water, I watched her closely. Her strength had returned. In a burst of joy, she leaped high into the air and spun around four times before crashing back into the sea. Neither Snapper nor I could spin so many times in a single leap.

For the first time, I asked how she became separated from her pod. Our dolphins never swam away from a pod member in trouble, but spinner dolphins might be different.

The pictures she sent frightened me. I saw hundreds of spinner dolphins frolicking in the water. Beneath them swam a school of tuna. Suddenly, small boats came from every side. They herded the dolphins toward a large ship, just as dolphins herd a school of herrings they intend to eat. As soon as the dolphins reached the ship's side, another boat left the ship's stern, pulling an enormous net.

The net spread out in the water, engulfing the tuna

and most of the dolphins. Slowly, the circle of net was pulled back into the ship. As the last of the net rose out of the sea, many of the dolphins escaped over the side. Caught fast in the mesh, others did not. In the confusion, Sea Fan became separated from the other dolphins. She swam hard and fast, fleeing the humans and their boats.

She swam all through the night and all the next day. She swam without stopping to eat or sleep. She never saw the drift net spread across the sea. She hit the net so hard that it knocked the breath out of her. She was caught fast.

I whistled signals of comfort to let her know she was safe now. Although I sounded brave, I wondered whether we would be able to stay a safe distance from humans who wanted to kill or capture us.

While we played, the tide had gone out. Far ahead of us stretched a wide, sloping beach, its wet sand glistening in the sun. Small wavelets broke lazily along its length, gently tumbling scattered shells. Sandpipers ran back and forth at the water's edge, searching for their dinner.

We moved into deeper water and swam fast for a long time. There were no inlets on this part of the coast, so we stayed far from the shore. For the first time in several days, we felt safe.

The sun moved across the sky and began to dip

toward the water. It was a big red ball when we met the boat.

When I saw the boat, I whistled a warning.

As usual, Snapper paid no attention. He saw the boat before I did and swam straight for it. In the highest of spirits, he surfed on the bow wave, laughing and playing. Snapper leaped high and dove deep, to please himself and the humans who were watching from the deck.

Again and again Sea Fan and I whistled Snapper's name. He ignored us. I can't explain his foolishness. He had surfed safely on the bow wave of the boat that captured White Fang. I suppose he remembered that. He often forgot bad things, and he must have forgotten our encounters with the whale killers and the otter hunters.

Snapper was putting us all in danger. Angry at his reckless actions, I swam toward him. Sea Fan hesitated, then followed. Together, we could grab his flippers and pull him back.

Just as we reached the bow, Snapper dove deep and swam to the other side. Before Sea Fan and I could follow him, the boat made a slow turn. A net flew out and settled in the water. We were trapped. Frantically, we swam back and forth. There was no way out.

The net drew around us. Sea Fan began to struggle.

She thrashed so violently that I was afraid she would become tangled in the mesh and drown.

"Still. Lie still," I signaled.

She stopped fighting and lay still as death.

The net rose through the water, holding us fast. It went up into the air and over the side of the boat. It moved over the deck and suddenly opened, dumping us into a tank of water.

As I lay in the shallow water, afraid to move, I heard Snapper's whistle rising from the sea. I did not answer. My heart was beating fast. So was Sea Fan's. We waited for the humans to kill us with a long bar.

Two of the humans leaned over the tank. Their tentacles were empty. They made soothing noises. One of them got into the water with us and rubbed our backs and sides.

They were not going to kill us. Not yet.

My heart slowed down. I took a deep breath. I whistled softly to Sea Fan to keep up her courage. She whimpered, but her heart slowed, too.

For a long time, nothing happened. Then the boat stopped. The humans lifted us out of the tank and covered us with something solid, but wet. It felt like a thin slice of a giant sponge. They packed ice under our flippers and put us in a shiny metal boat that had fins and a tail.

There was a roaring noise, and the boat with fins left the ground. It flew through the air like a bird, so I decided that's what it was. After a long time, the metal bird landed and we were put in a small open boat that rolled over the land. All this time, the same two humans stayed with us. Not once did they reach for a metal bar or a shooting stick.

10

As the boat that carried us rolled over the land, I found little to comfort me. Snapper was alone in the vast ocean. Sea Fan and I were captives. I had not found my brother. I had not discovered a place where the herd could move. I had failed in every way. Never had I felt so sad as I did that day.

Sea Fan tried to cheer me up. She laid her flipper across my back. She sent pictures of us swimming together in a lagoon.

I didn't believe her. Perhaps the humans intended to eat us. Since only live food is good to eat, they might be keeping us alive until they got hungry. I whistled with alarm at the thought, but kept it to myself. I didn't want to frighten Sea Fan.

At last we stopped. More humans appeared. They clustered around us.

A human whose head was covered with short yellow hair held a thing like a strand of kelp along the side of my head, first between my eye and my blowhole, then from the tip of my beak to a spot below my flipper. Next Yellow Hair circled my body with the thing. Each time the position of the thing changed, Yellow Hair made a noise and another of the humans pulled a small stick across a flat thing.

Suddenly, I felt a sharp pain in my fluke. I looked over my shoulder and saw that one of the humans had stuck something sharp into me. When the human pulled it out, the thing was full of blood.

At last the humans slid me out of the box. Something pulled me high off the pad and moved me out over water. As I swayed back and forth in the air, all my stomachs began to churn.

The thing dropped me into the water. As the water rushed over me, I felt light and cool instead of heavy and hot as I had ever since the humans pulled me out of the sea.

It felt good to swim again. But when I scanned with my farsensor, echoes bounced back from every side. The sounds made me dizzy, and I blundered into the tank wall. I could use my farsensor only if I kept the beam tight and scanned at short range.

By the time I had figured this out, Sea Fan splashed down beside me. Before she could make the same mistake, I let her know that wide beams were a bad idea.

When she felt better, we swam along the bottom, circling the tank. There was no way out. Three sides of the enclosure were solid. The fourth side was made of a heavy metal mesh. Through it, I could see a narrow channel and, beyond, the mesh of another enclosure.

The humans threw us several fish, but they were dead. I had never eaten dead fish in my life. Neither had Sea Fan. Although we were hungry, we let the fish settle to the bottom. When we refused to eat, the humans left us alone all night. By morning, I was so hungry that I was ready to eat anything. Even kelp sounded good.

At last a human appeared. Yellow Hair knelt at the water's edge and held a fish toward me. The fish did not move. It was dead. I swam away.

Yellow Hair wiggled the fish. I swam back to the edge of the tank. Rolling on my side, I peered closely at the fish. It was still dead, but its silver sides glistened. My hunger welled up. Ravenous, I surged forward to get the fish. At the last minute, my fear was too great. I veered away from Yellow Hair's outstretched tentacle and swam off, still hungry.

The human shook its head. It made a small, unhappy sound. Then it threw the fish into the water. It landed near me. I held it in my mouth and touched it gently with my tongue. To my surprise, it tasted good. I swallowed the fish and was ready for more. I swam to the water's edge, held my head out of the water, and opened my jaws wide. Yellow Hair tossed me a fish, then another.

Sea Fan hung back. She swam up and down, watching us out of one eye. I carried a fish over to her, but she moved her head away from the dead anchovy.

"It's good," I whistled. "Eat." I tossed the fish into the air.

It hit the water and began to sink. Sea Fan glanced toward Yellow Hair, hesitated, then scooped up the anchovy. She flipped it around so the fins wouldn't stick in her throat and swallowed. Her eyes brightened, and she swam back with me for more.

We were so busy filling our bellies that we paid no attention to loud splashing at the other end of the pool. Then wild whistles filled the air.

The whistles were name signals repeated again and again. "Coral! Coral! Coral! Silver! Silver! Silver!"

I had just opened my mouth to grab a fish. I snapped my jaws shut, twisted about, and bounded into the air. Then I raced toward the other end of the tank, where my brother Silver had entered the water.

When we met, we leaped high into the air, calling each other's name again and again. We dove to the bottom, touched beaks, then raced to the surface, breaking into the air once more. My heart leaped as high as our surging bodies. I had found my brother.

We swam around the enclosure three times, our

sides touching and our flippers intertwined. When I calmed down, I noticed two other dolphins in our water. One was a female, and the other was a young child, little more than a baby.

I stopped near them, whistled my name, then the signal for question.

Silver and the young female answered with a single voice. The female dolphin was Spray, and her child was Silver's son. Spray was born at this place, which she called "Paradise Cove." When Silver was captured, the humans put him into her enclosure and they soon fell in love. Their son, Flasher, was a year old. When I found my brother, I also found a new sister and a nephew. It was a joyous occasion.

Silver was so happy he began to whistle a beautiful song. He used all our name signals, weaving them together in an intricate melody. The music rose and swelled. The rest of us floated in silence, entranced by the lovely sounds.

The humans paid no attention to the song, which surprised me. Later I discovered that the creatures are almost deaf. They can hear only coarse, deep sounds. Their disability cuts them off from much of the world's beauty. It also makes it very difficult to communicate with them.

11

The channel outside our enclosure was connected to the sea. Twice a day, our water grew deep as the tide came in, and, twice a day, it grew shallow again. At low tide, there was still enough water to dive, but not very far.

At low tide the first evening, I told Silver about my mission. He was surprised to hear that Father and the other males had sent Snapper and me off to look for him. He clapped his jaws angrily at the thought of leaving Paradise Cove and going back to the frosty waters of Glacier Strait. He was happy and had no wish to go.

His reply disappointed me. By now I knew that the humans were not going to kill us, but I still did not trust them. And I worried about Snapper, swimming by himself among the sharks and orcas that frequented the coast.

Spray worried about Snapper, too. She hoped that he would be captured and join us. Paradise Cove was a good place to live, she told me. These humans were not like the ones we had met on our journey south. Life was good here, and no harm could come to us.

I bobbed my head at her and swam away. There was plenty of food at this place, but no room to leap and frolic as we did in the sea. To protect ourselves from the booming echoes, we had to whistle and click as softly as we could. It was a strange life.

Within a few weeks, life got even stranger. One morning Yellow Hair got into the enclosure with us. Once she was in the water, I could use my farsensor and see inside her body. The echoes told me that she was female. Her insides were peculiar. Some of her organs were like those of a dolphin, but others were different. The human had a narrow throat and could swallow only tiny fish. She also had only a single stomach, instead of three like dolphins. I wondered how she was able to digest fish after she swallowed them.

Yellow Hair's problems didn't end there. When she swam through the water, her blowhole was on the wrong side of her head. That made it difficult for her to breathe. Her head was flat and had no sensing organ inside. She could never use echoes to locate objects in dark water or to look inside the creatures who swam there. She would not last long in the sea.

After swimming with us for a while, Yellow Hair sat on the edge of a platform at the end of the enclosure. Beside her were pails of glistening fish.

We were hungry and swam over, expecting to be fed. Instead, Yellow Hair lifted a tentacle, then dropped it. At once, Silver and Spray dove together, then leaped high into the air. Yellow Hair put something to her mouth, made a sharp, whistling sound, and tossed them each a fish.

At first I was puzzled. By watching Silver and Spray, I discovered that whenever the whistle blew, they got a fish. The whistle was a sign that the humans liked whatever Silver and Spray had done. Leaping in the air when Yellow Hair waved her tentacle was not a difficult task, and Sea Fan and I soon got fish for ourselves.

From that day, we had to work with the humans if we wanted any fish before the sun was high overhead. I suppose I should have resented having to work for my breakfast, but it was boring to swim all day in the same small space. While I watched for signals and listened for whistles, I was too busy to think about Snapper or about home.

Yellow Hair swam with us only once. After that, we worked with another human. This one was bigger than Yellow Hair, and he had black hair that clung to his head in tiny curls. Yellow Hair called him something that sounded like a seal barking. At first I thought it was "Ark!" but when I listened hard, I discovered his name signal was "Mark."

Mark taught us many tricks, and within a few weeks, we were part of the show. Twice a day we spun on our tails, jumped through hoops, tail-walked, and rang bells. Sea Fan and I had a special trick. When Mark gave a certain signal, we dove to the bottom, swam to opposite sides of the tank, then leaped high into the air. While we were still far above the water, we passed side by side, our bodies almost brushing. Spray said it was a beautiful sight.

Silver and Spray had a special trick, too. They swam together beneath a trainer with hair as red as a rosy rockfish. This trainer's hair stood up from his head, like the stiff spines of a sculpin. Red Hair was longer than Mark but thin.

Red Hair got into the tank, then stood up, with one fluke on Silver's back and the other on Spray's back. His tentacles were wrapped around a tether that ran to a bar held tightly in their jaws. Silver and Spray carried Red Hair around and around the tank. As they sped through the water, Red Hair waved to the crowd. The watching humans made loud noises of pleasure.

The trainers made happy sounds when we picked up their tricks after a few signals. They didn't know that Silver had told us what the different signals meant. So instead of working for days on a single trick, we polished off each one in a morning.

We could have done even better, but we enjoyed the extra fish. During our practice sessions, the trainer blew a whistle and fed us an anchovy or smelt each time we jumped or spun or tail-walked on cue. So we learned just slowly enough to keep the fish coming.

One stormy morning we were playing Hide-and-Seek with Flasher when a harsh whistle stopped our frolic. I whirled about and saw an enormous black and white shape burst into the air and fall heavily into the water on the other side of the channel. It made a loud crash, sending waves of water into our pool. The humans had brought in an orca.

It was not just any orca. When it leaped again, I saw that a moon-shaped piece of flesh was gone from its dorsal fin. Our new neighbor was White Fang! Sometime during the night he had been turned into the enclosure across from us.

Spray whistled to Flasher and drew him close. I dove to the bottom and stayed there until I ran out of breath. Even though I knew White Fang could not reach us, a shiver of fear ran down my spine.

Silver responded quickly. He raised his head above the water and whistled a greeting. To send the sound through the air, he had to keep his blowhole open, which we never do when talking underwater.

White Fang wanted to know if we were prisoners, too. He sounded more sad than mean.

Silver whistled and sent pictures showing how much he liked life at Paradise Cove. He let White Fang know that we were safe here, protected from guns and nets and sharks. He could not resist adding that we were also protected from orcas. It took him a long time to make the orca understand.

Worn out with the effort of calling through the air, Silver took a big breath and dove to the bottom. There he rolled over on his back and rested.

Beneath the water Silver could not hear White Fang's reply. But I heard every whistle.

The sounds came slowly, one by one. "Dead fish," he signaled. "No room to swim. No room to dive. No family. No friends. Alone. Alone."

His voice had lost its fierceness. White Fang was miserable. I suppose I should have felt sorry for him. But secretly I rejoiced in his gloom. It served him right.

After a while, we realized that we were in no danger from the orca. Flasher emerged from the safety of Spray's flipper. We paid no more attention to White Fang. For the rest of the morning, we frolicked, teaching young Flasher some of the games we played in Glacier Strait. While we romped, Spray hovered nearby, keeping watch on her son. When Flasher grew tired, he rested beside her.

Flasher was just learning to eat fish. He preferred

Spray's milk to solid food. At feeding time, he often played with the silvery smelt instead of swallowing it. Sometimes he caught the tiny fish that swam in through the chain-link gate, but he treated them like toys. He would snatch up a fish and toss it into the air. When it swam away, he chased after it and tossed it again.

His antics fascinated Sea Fan. Safe from the dangers of the open sea, she had lost most of her fears. She no longer trembled when a trainer appeared, and she enjoyed performing in the shows. Sea Fan became Flasher's second mother and often cared for him when Silver and Spray swam together.

I still tested the wire mesh each night, hoping to find a way out of our enclosure. But life was so easy at Paradise Cove that days sometimes passed before I thought of the troubles in Glacier Strait or wondered whether Snapper was safe.

12

As the days went by, the commotion around White Fang's enclosure increased. Red Hair and Mark worked with him every morning, trying to teach him tricks. The huge orca wanted no part of the show. Sometimes he became so angry at their attempts that he showed his sharp teeth and shook his head at the trainers. He thrashed his big tail or slapped at them with his flippers. They were afraid to get into the tank with him.

The trainers often spoke about their problems with the orca, but it was hard to figure out what they meant. Humans send only low sounds and drag out each one. It takes them forever to exchange a message.

We recognized some of the noises they made. We knew their sounds for one another's name signals and the sounds that meant "fish," "yes," and "no." We knew their sounds for each of us. They called me "Nicki," and they called Silver "Romeo." Sea Fan was "Sandy," Spray was "Violet," and Flasher was "Spunky." Each day we picked up new signals, but we learned more from watching their bodies than from listening to them talk.

Every day they argued about what they should do with White Fang, whom they called "Monstro." Yellow Hair seemed to be mother of the trainer pod. Her body stiff with rage, she shook her tentacle at Mark.

Yellow Hair wanted him to spend more time teaching White Fang. She wanted him to cut back on the orca's fish until he started to work. Mark moved his head back and forth and made the "no" sound. He felt that it was cruel to force the unhappy orca to perform.

Each morning he took buckets of fish to White Fang's enclosure. He was trying to persuade the giant orca to leap out of the water and hit a big orange ball with his forehead. Mark would toss the ball into the water and wait for White Fang to move toward it. But White Fang ignored it. When Mark threw the ball, White Fang no longer reared up in anger or slapped the water with his flukes. Instead, he turned his back on the trainers and moved to the other side of the enclosure.

As the days wore on, my joy over White Fang's plight slipped away. He lost interest in everything and spent his time drifting or swimming in slow circles. He never answered our whistles. At night, he groaned and moaned in the dark.

Anyone could see how sad White Fang was. Yet every morning Red Hair and Mark worked with the orca, trying to get him to toss a ball or jump through a hoop. He didn't earn a single smelt. Twice a day, when no one was looking, Mark fed him pails of fish. But White Fang had lost his appetite and ate only a few. He grew thinner each day.

One dark, moonless night the pod was resting, only half awake. Sounds rippled down the channel, but I was the only one who heard them. I swam over to the chain-link gate and sent out a spray of sound. The returning echoes revealed a human in fins and mask. It was Mark. In his tentacle was a bag.

He swam to White Fang's enclosure and opened the bag. From it he pulled a metal tool and began to work on the chain-link fence. When he moved the tool with his tentacles, it bit deeply into the strand of metal. Each cut made a sharp ping that sounded like a dolphin using its farsensor.

Mark started at the top, cutting one link after another. Then he worked underwater. Again and again, he took a deep breath, dove, and cut a link in the gate. First he worked along on one side of the fence, then on the other.

When he severed the last link, the section of fence fell over. It crashed through the water, sending up spray. Before Mark could swim away, the section of fence landed on top of him. It shoved him backward, pinning him to the bottom of the channel.

Sensor echoes showed Mark struggling to get away, but the fence was heavy. It did not stir. Then it moved a few inches off the bottom.

Mark tried to wriggle free, but he was caught. His shirt was snagged on a jagged edge of the fence. Shut behind my own fence, I could do nothing to help him. In another minute he would drown.

Mark twisted and turned. At last he managed to squirm out of his shirt. Now he could move, but the fence still weighed him down.

As I watched helplessly, Mark lay still. Then, using his last bit of air, he drew his flukes up beneath him and kicked hard. The gate rose a little. Quickly, Mark wiggled free and shot to the surface. His head burst out of the water. For a long time, he held on to the wall and gulped air.

White Fang swam over to the opening. He looked through the hole in the fence. I could hear clicks and pings as the orca examined the opening and the channel with his farsensor. For some reason, he did not like what he saw. He did not enter the channel.

"Go, Monstro," Mark urged. "Go! Go!"

White Fang did not understand. He thought it was a trick.

Mark took a deep breath and swam into White

Fang's enclosure. My farsensor told me that Mark's muscles were tight with fear at what the giant orca might do. I could taste his fear in the water.

Mark grabbed one of White Fang's flippers and tugged. The orca did not move. Mark tugged again. White Fang clapped his jaws to warn the trainer. The orca was angry. In another moment he would bite with his cruel teeth.

I don't know whether I was trying to protect Mark or help White Fang. Maybe I hoped to do both. But I found myself whistling as loudly as I could. "Forget human," I signaled. "Swim. Swim away. Free."

At last White Fang heard my call. He stopped threatening Mark. "Free?" he whistled.

"Yes! Yes!" I whistled. "Go! Safe!"

The orca slipped through the opening and turned toward the sea. In a moment, he was gone.

The channel was a short one. Before long I heard excited whistles. White Fang had reached the sea.

As I listened, I realized that the orca was calling to me. His clicks and whistles thanked me, told me he was going home, and said that he would never eat another dolphin. "Salmon and seals," he signaled. "Salmon and seals. No dolphins."

I could hardly believe his message. Maybe orcas were not as evil as I had thought. White Fang was grateful, and he intended to do something about it.

Once he reached home waters, perhaps I could stop worrying about the dolphins in Glacier Strait. I whistled with happiness.

By now Mark had caught his breath. He looked across the channel. He sent some sounds, but all I caught was "Nicki."

I replied with my name whistle, "Coral! Coral!" I whistled as loudly as I could, hoping that he would free me, too.

Mark made happy sounds and swam over to our gate. He stuck his hand through the chain link and stroked my head, just in front of the blowhole. He did not use the cutting tool on my fence.

Mark swam back down the channel. Sadly, I watched him go. I wondered if I ever would be free again. As he moved out of sensor range, I thought about the way Mark had risked his life to save White Fang. I decided that some humans were as decent as dolphins.

13

The next morning Yellow Hair discovered the broken fence and the empty pen. She made loud, angry sounds. The way she held her body when Mark was around told me that she suspected him of freeing White Fang. But there was no way to prove it.

When Mark fed us that evening, he gave me extra fish and caressed my side. Over and over, he said "Nicki" along with a lot of other soft, friendly sounds. I could tell that he was pleased with me. When he sat on the edge, dangling his flukes in the water, I rubbed up against them to tell him that I liked him, too.

Before long, Mark came to our enclosure most evenings. Until then, he had spent his free time with the big, gray bottlenose dolphins in one of the other enclosures. He slipped into the water and swam with us. Diving and splashing, we swam side by side, spun in circles, and played dolphin games. Mark was almost like another dolphin, except that he could not swim fast or stay long beneath the water.

When he grew tired, he lay on an air-filled mat and

floated beside us. Sometimes he spent most of the night drifting with us. On evenings when he did not appear, I felt sad and lonely. It was an odd way to feel about a human.

I certainly didn't feel that way about the other humans, especially Yellow Hair. From time to time, she taught us new stunts. Our pod learned to form a large ring on the surface of the water, each putting a beak just behind the next dolphin's flukes. Then we swam on our backs, slapping the water with our flukes as we circled the performance tank as fast as we could go. It made lots of noise and people laughed. Yellow Hair called it "motorboating."

One morning, Mark took Sea Fan and me into the performance tank by ourselves. I had learned to hit a ball toward a goal placed at one end of the tank, and so had Sea Fan. Today there was a goal at each end.

Mark threw the ball into the water and watched. I let Sea Fan take the ball. She batted it toward the goal at her end of the tank. When it struck, she looked at Mark and waited for her fish. Nothing happened.

Mark tossed the ball again. This time I batted the ball while Sea Fan watched. Still no fish. Mark was waiting for something else to happen.

Again the ball hit the water. Sea Fan leaped on top

of it. It sank beneath the surface, then shot high into the air. Mark did not move.

The next time he threw the ball, I turned on my back, swam under it, and balanced it on my beak. Then I swam backward around the tank, carrying the ball. Mark was as still as a stone. This was becoming difficult.

The ball skipped across the surface. I decided to try something new. "Race you for it," I whistled, and darted toward the ball. Sea Fan reached the ball first and pushed it toward her goal. I dove, came up on the other side of the ball, and tossed it over her head. Then I grabbed it between my teeth and hurled it toward the goal behind her. It hit with a loud smack.

Mark blew his whistle and tossed fish to both of us.

I decided that Mark wanted us to fight over the ball. I told Sea Fan to pretend the ball was a piece of kelp.

That made the game easy. We tussled over the ball until the sun moved above the palm trees. By then we were full of fish and ready to go back to our enclosure. Within a week, our new game was part of the show.

The performance tank had glass sides so humans could watch us underwater. They always made loud, happy noises when Silver and Spray did a special trick. Together, they swam through a series of six hoops under the water, weaving back and forth. The trick ended with a great leap through a seventh hoop suspended in the air.

One afternoon something happened. Silver and Spray leaped through the last hoop and swam to Red Hair for their reward. Just as he tossed them each a fish, a shiny object came hurtling out of the crowd.

Spray was hungry. Eager to get her fish before it hit the water, she jumped toward it. The smelt crossed paths with the shiny object in midair, and Spray grabbed the object instead. It was a silver ball. Before she realized what she had done, she had swallowed it.

"Tasted awful," she whistled. She dived to scoop her fish off the bottom, and the show went on.

Within a day or two, Spray felt sick. She couldn't eat. She didn't feel like playing. She asked Sea Fan to take care of Flasher and went off alone to the deep end of the enclosure.

Silver was worried. He joined her, and they swam in slow circles, their bodies touching. As we watched, Silver broke away. With his beak almost touching Spray's side, Silver swayed his head to and fro, sending out a rapid burst of sound pings. He inspected her from head to tail.

When he finished, he was more worried than ever. Sensor echoes showed that the metal ball Spray had swallowed was lodged at the entrance to her first stomach. It closed her throat so that food could not pass.

Except for Flasher, who was chasing tiny fish, we gathered around Spray.

Sea Fan sent pictures of herself spitting up fish after she had overeaten. She wanted Spray to try to spit out the ball.

Spray signaled "No" in a weak voice. She had already tried to get the ball out.

"Try again," signaled Sea Fan.

Spray made an effort to cough up the ball, but nothing happened.

I had an idea. I sent a picture of me bumping Spray's stomach as hard as I could. Then I sent a picture of the ball flying into her throat so she could get rid of it.

Spray didn't think it would work.

"Try!" boomed Silver. He signaled that this was important.

His message was clear. If we did not dislodge the ball, Spray would die.

I turned away from Spray and suddenly slapped her hard with my flukes, right behind the place where the ball rested.

She winced, but the ball did not move.

"Again?" I whistled.

"Again," signaled Silver. He let me know that he was afraid to try it himself. He feared that he was so strong that he might rupture Spray's stomach.

Once more I drew back my flukes and smacked Spray in the stomach.

The ball stayed in place.

We decided to call the humans. With their sharp metal sticks and their white pills, they made sick dolphins well. Perhaps they could get the ball out of Spray's stomach.

We began whistling as loudly as we could, using only low tones so the humans could hear us.

After a while, Red Hair wandered over to the enclosure. "What's wrong?" he asked. "Did a shark come calling?"

Silver raised his head out of the water and jerked it toward Spray. He jerked it again.

Red Hair decided that Silver was angry. "Cool it, Romeo," he said. He scratched the back of his leg with the tip of his fluke. "Maybe the girls just aren't interested in you today." He laughed and walked away.

"Stupid!" signaled Silver. Then he made the sign for many humans, saying that all humans were stupid.

We tried whistling again, but no one came. The humans left us alone the rest of the morning. Spray did not get better.

Just before showtime, Mark came out to open the gates so we could swim into the performance tank. We whistled, and he whistled back, trying to imitate a dolphin. It was a bad imitation. He sounded like a gull.

I swam to the water's edge, whistling all the way, and jerked my head at Spray.

Mark knelt beside me. "What is it, Nicki?" he said. "You're trying to tell me something."

Silver and Sea Fan joined me. The three of us whistled and bobbed our heads in Spray's direction. Then Silver left and swam around Spray, whistling wildly as he circled her.

Mark scowled and shook his head. "I don't know what you're saying."

We tried again, but he still didn't understand.

The gates were open, but no one went through.

"Come on, gang," he said. "Showtime!"

We looked at one another.

Spray signaled for us to go ahead. She would do her best to carry out her tricks. Together, we moved into the performance tank.

At Yellow Hair's signal, we got in place for the motorboating stunt. Spray was in front of me. She swam so slowly that the circle barely moved. Her tail smacks were so weak that they barely rippled the water.

Yellow Hair shook her head. She was angry. "Why won't they move?" she said. She gave the signal again, but no one swam faster.

Yellow Hair gave up. She signaled for the first jumping stunt. Sea Fan and I began our leaps, which ended with our crossing in midair. While we performed, Red Hair and Mark placed the hoops for Silver and Spray's first trick.

The humans were still hitting their tentacles together and making happy noises when Red Hair stepped into position and signaled for the hoop trick.

Spray started to swim, then stopped. "Can't," she signaled. She hung back in the corner of the tank.

"Let me," signaled Sea Fan. She had watched every day while Spray performed and knew just what to do. At Silver's side, she swam through the chain of hoops, weaving from one side to the other. The trick was half over before Red Hair realized that Sea Fan had taken Spray's place.

At the signal for Spray's next trick, it was my turn. Red Hair jumped into the tank and waited. Staying beside Silver, I swam along the bottom, made a large circle, and scooted under Red Hair, who had drawn up his knees. He placed a fluke just behind my blowhole and in front of my dorsal fin. He was heavy, and I sank beneath his weight. Tensing my muscles, I moved level with Silver.

Red Hair tossed the bar into the water. I bit down on my end of it, and we were off. I kept my left eye on Silver, who whistled cues to me as we swam. We circled the tank three times, while the audience cheered and clapped.

By the end of the show, the trainers realized that something was wrong with Spray. As soon as we returned to our enclosure, they placed her on a canvas sling and took her away in one of the land ships.

14

Days passed. Silver no longer greeted the morning with songs of joy. At first light, he swam to the edge of the enclosure and stared hopefully toward the cave with straight sides where the humans cared for sick and injured animals. But no land ship rolled in our direction.

Silver paid little attention to the rest of us. He even ignored Flasher, who whistled plaintively for his mother. When Flasher nudged his father's side, Silver seemed not to feel the little dolphin's beak.

The rest of us tried to cheer up Flasher, but sadness had settled over our pod. Our games ended quickly. No one felt like tossing a ball or chasing the bright fish that swam in from the sea. We still swam with Mark when he came into the water. He seemed to understand our sorrow and treated us gently. While we swam together, Silver drifted aimlessly and watched us splashing about.

With Spray gone, Flasher got no milk. He ate some fish, but not enough to keep a tuna alive. He stayed healthy because the trainers fed him several times each day. They put a black tube down his throat and poured in a mixture of ground fish and water. Flasher struggled so hard when he felt the tube in his mouth that it took three trainers to get a meal into his stomach.

Most of the day Flasher stayed at Sea Fan's side. Late at night he whistled sad sounds. It had been a long time since I had thought about my family, but his sorrowful songs put pictures of home in my head. I missed Mother and Urchin and Father and hoped that White Fang had reached their waters — and that he had kept his word. I wondered whether the new baby had arrived. I thought how Urchin would feel if something happened to Mother. I thought about Snapper, too, but not as often.

One terrible day Silver realized that Spray was never coming back. We had just returned from the performance tank and were waiting for Mark to bring us our dinner.

While jumping and diving with Flasher, I surfaced to breathe. With my head above the water, I detected an unusual noise in the distance. The sound grew louder.

Silver heard it, too. He rose high in the water. Turning his head, he looked in the direction of the sound.

I followed his gaze. Against the glare of the afternoon sun, I made out the shape of a land ship. It looked like the one that had carried Spray to the cave for sick animals.

Silver whistled for joy. "Spray!" he said. "Coming home!" He jumped again and again, watching the land ship's approach.

The land ship drew near our enclosure and slowed. Silver leaped into the air and whistled Spray's name.

Without stopping, the land ship rumbled past. It rolled onto the pier that jutted out into the lagoon.

A shudder passed over Silver's body. A great bellow echoed across the park. Silver made a towering leap and crashed down in the water. Huge waves washed across the walkway.

"Dead," he whistled. "Dead. My Spray. Dead." He made sounds of pain, then whirled about and swam across the enclosure at top speed. He smashed into the wall.

Silver was stunned. He shook his head, turned, and headed for the opposite wall.

"Stop!" I whistled. "Silver, stop!"

Silver did not answer. He seemed not to hear. He hurtled across the pool, seeing nothing.

Sea Fan whistled in distress.

Directly in Silver's path floated Flasher, who stared at his father but seemed unable to move. In another moment, Silver's enormous body would crush him against the wall.

I could not make a sound.

Suddenly, a sleek shape sped through the water. Pushing me aside, Sea Fan leaped on top of Flasher. Her weight pushed the little dolphin deep into the water. Hurtling through the space where Flasher had been, Silver's massive head struck Sea Fan just below the dorsal fin.

Squeaking in protest, Flasher rose to the surface. His blowhole whooshed as air rushed into his lungs. After floundering for a moment, he swam into the corner, where the solid wall met the fence.

Sea Fan was not so lucky. She rolled over and lay still. Her eyes were closed. She began to sink. Dolphins must think about each breath they take. If Sea Fan did not come to, she would die.

I had to act quickly. With a strong stroke of my flukes, I dove under Sea Fan. I flipped her onto her stomach. Moving my body under her, I pushed her to the surface. I held her with her blowhole above water. Still she did not breathe.

Time was running out. Without thinking, I turned my head and bit hard. My teeth raked across Sea Fan's skin, drawing blood.

Sea Fan's eye flickered. Her blowhole opened, and she took a ragged breath. She was still groggy, so I supported her. The task would have been easier with help, but Silver made no attempt to assist me.

As soon as Sea Fan could swim on her own, I darted toward Silver. With angry whistles and a burst of intense jaw-clapping, I sprayed him with sound pictures of a dead Silver and a lonely Flasher. I told him that killing himself would not bring Spray back.

Silver looked at me. His eye was dull. He was still wobbly from his collisions with the wall. "Gone," he signaled. "My Spray. Gone forever. Why live?"

"Spray gone," I signaled. "Flasher here." Quickly, I sent pictures of Silver nearly crashing into his son, the collision with Sea Fan, and her slipping to the bottom, unconscious.

Silver blinked. Slowly, he grasped the meaning of my whistles. "No more," he signaled. "No more death."

With Spray gone, Silver became a different dolphin. He didn't join our daily games. He never sang. He said little to any of us. He still performed, but he no longer enjoyed it. His jumps were not as high, his spins were ragged, and his timing was off.

The trainers worried about him. Red Hair often sat at the water's edge and talked to him. Mark invited him to join in our evening frolics. Silver avoided them, just as he avoided the other trainers. Whenever a trainer came near, he swam to the far side of the tank.

Then Silver began to spoil the show. Instead of swimming through the hoops, he grabbed them in his jaws and tore them loose from the floor of the tank. When Red Hair climbed into the tank for their stunt, Silver dashed up beneath the trainer and shoved hard. Unable to keep his balance, Red Hair fell over and dropped the lines. As Red Hair came to the surface, Silver swung around. With a blow of his flukes, he hit the trainer over the head.

Within a few days, Silver was taken out of the show. When we left the enclosure to perform, Silver stayed behind with Flasher. Sea Fan and I learned most of Silver's tricks, but it was not the same.

Silver so loved to perform that we worked hard to keep up with him. Without him to inspire us, we missed our cues and shortened our leaps. It wasn't fun anymore.

15

During the night, trailing clouds appeared and a wind rattled the palm trees. Rain began just before dawn and fell steadily all morning. Water soaked the seats around the performance tank. There were no shows. We were left to ourselves.

About midday, the rain stopped and the sun shone weakly. Red Hair came sloshing through the puddles. In each tentacle he carried a bright bucket filled with fish. He squatted down on the platform at the edge of the tank.

We crowded around. Flasher squirmed his way to the front. He raised his head above the water and squeaked for food. By now he ate his share of fish. The black tube had been gone for many suns.

One at a time, Red Hair doled out fish until the pails were empty. Silver, who was still hungry, whistled for more. Red Hair turned the pails upside down, then held out his empty tentacles to show that he had no more fish.

One of the empty pails sat on the edge of the platform. Silver swam over, thrust his tail into the air, and, with his flukes, swept the pail into the water. He tucked the pail under his flipper. Trailing bubbles, he carried it to the bottom.

Red Hair laughed and shook his head. He shucked off his sandals and dove into the tank. With two strokes, he reached the bottom. He snatched the pail from Silver and started back to the surface.

Silver wanted to keep his new toy. Sputtering with anger, he followed the trainer. Silver jerked his head and clapped his jaws, but Red Hair kept swimming for the side of the tank.

With a burst of speed, Silver passed Red Hair and turned quickly. Opening his mouth wide, Silver grabbed the trainer's head between his jaws and pulled Red Hair to the platform.

Red Hair let go of the pail. He scrambled out of the water. Blood streamed from his ear, where Silver's teeth had torn the flesh. Holding his hand against the gash, Red Hair ran off.

Silver stuck his beak into the pail and tossed it in the air. It struck the water with a satisfying splash.

Sea Fan and Flasher watched him with wide eyes. None of us had ever harmed a trainer.

I asked Silver what he was trying to do. Then I sent our signal for a rogue dolphin, one that was out of control and as dangerous to other dolphins as a hungry killer whale. Such dolphins were cast out from their herd and lived alone in the sea.

"Mine," signaled Silver. "My pail." He felt that he had warned Red Hair and that the trainer should not have tried to retrieve the pail. He swam once around the tank, then came back to the rest of us. "Not hurt," he signaled. "Not hurt. Red Hair out of water."

Sea Fan was sad. She whistled the signal for bad behavior, then sent a picture of Silver gradually turning into an orca.

Silver pretended he didn't hear her. He tossed the pail a few more times, caught it on his flukes, and rolled it down his back. Then he swam off. The pail sank slowly to the bottom.

When Silver reached the corner, he stopped. He floated upright in the water, his head and chest in the air. He was warning us not to come near.

I swam over to him, but stayed well out of reach. He was stronger than I was. I whistled, asking him what was wrong.

He slapped the water with his flippers. "Don't like this place," he signaled. "Don't like humans." He sent a picture of humans killing Spray.

My whistle blasted through the water. "No! No!" I sent pictures of the trainers trying to save Spray, then pictures of the trainers feeding Flasher.

Although Silver knew that humans had saved Flasher's life, he had pushed the memory away. He just didn't care anymore. He didn't care about anything. With bleak whistles, he signaled that it didn't make any difference.

I wanted to comfort him, but I could think of nothing.

Just then Mark came down the walkway. His face was grim and worried. He sat on the side of the pool and dangled his flukes in the water. He looked toward Silver and began making sounds. I couldn't understand everything, but he seemed to be asking Silver what was wrong and warning him of trouble.

Silver looked the other way. He did not leave his corner.

I swam over to Mark and rubbed against him. He stroked my side but did not look at me. He sent more sounds to Silver.

After a time, Silver swam toward us. He turned on his side and drifted by, gazing steadily at Mark. When Mark stretched out a tentacle to touch him, Silver whirled and fled.

Mark was patient. He made more soothing sounds. The next time Silver swam by, Mark kept his tentacles close against his own body.

Silver swam back and forth, watching Mark closely.

The big dolphin seemed calm, but the sensor echoes told me that his muscles were stiff and tight. He might do anything.

After a while Mark pulled on his mask and fins and slipped into the water. He kept his tentacles at his sides as he matched Silver's movements. They were about a dolphin length apart.

Silver speeded up. He passed Mark, turned, and came back. As he went by, he sent a warning sensor blast. It was loud enough to stun a school of fish. It meant, "Get out of the water."

Mark felt the buzz. He stopped short and began to tread water. He did not realize that he was in danger.

I swam to him. Giving an explosive whistle, I nudged his side, trying to shove him to the platform so he could climb out. He didn't understand.

Silver dove to the bottom and came up with the pail hanging on his beak. He shook his head and sent the pail flying.

Mark must have thought that the pail toss was an invitation to play. He swam across the pool and scooped up the pail. Mark whirled about in the water, and his arm muscles tensed. He was ready to throw the pail back to Silver when the dolphin struck.

Silver raced toward Mark and butted him from behind. It was a solid blow, but not hard enough to injure him. Mark sank below the surface. He did not panic.

Instead, he reversed direction and began swimming underwater toward the platform.

Silver was not finished. He rushed after Mark, catching him with two strokes of his strong tail. He placed his beak in the small of Mark's back and pushed steadily downward. The pair sank to the bottom. Silver pinned the trainer facedown on the floor of the tank.

Mark was a strong swimmer, but he had started his race for the platform with half-empty lungs. Pulling up his legs, he shoved at Silver with all his might. Silver did not move.

Without a whistle, the rest of us dove to help Mark. We tried to push Silver off the trainer's body, but he did not budge.

Mark was running out of air. Behind his mask, his brown eyes were wide with fear.

Still Silver did not move. He held Mark firm. Then Flasher, whistling wildly, came charging up. He rammed his father hard in the side, just below the eye.

Silver was so surprised that he raised his head. Mark squirmed free and shot to the surface. Silver did not follow.

Before dark, five trainers moved Silver to White Fang's old enclosure.

16

For several days, Silver sulked in the far corner of his new enclosure, coming out only to eat. Then he began hovering around the gate that faced our pool across the channel. With sorrowful eyes, he watched us leap and splash together. When Flasher swam near the gate, Silver always whistled to him, but his whistles were so sad they broke my heart.

From time to time, we signaled back and forth. Silver denied doing anything wrong. He blamed the trainers for his lonely life. That made me even more unhappy. I knew that as long as Silver was angry with the trainers, he would not behave. And as long as he misbehaved, he had no hope of rejoining the pod.

The daily shows went on each afternoon without us. Bottlenose dolphins from another tank replaced our pod. Twice a day, at showtime, we heard their splashes and the shouts of watching humans. I missed the excitement and hoped that when Silver calmed down we would perform again.

On a morning when the sun lay golden on the water, a group of strange humans came to our pool. Their bodies were covered with white garments — even the tops of their heads. The strangers made noises to Yellow Hair, who made noises back. Then they left.

The next day Mark brought a new trainer to our pool. This trainer was female and smaller than Yellow Hair. Her brown hair was woven into a long rope that hung down her back. When Mark called her, he made a noise that sounded like the wind blowing over the sea. We decided that was her name, so we called her "Soooh."

Soooh worked with me first. She put a flat, round thing into the water. It had a hole in the center. It floated in front of me. The sound of a bell echoed through the water, and I poked the thing with my beak. Soooh blew her whistle and gave me a fish.

The next time I had to stick my beak into the hole before I got a fish. Then I had to swim across the pool to her, with the ring hanging around my beak. Finally, she tossed a different ring into the water. This one was heavy. It sank to the bottom. I dove after it, poked my beak through the hole, and brought it back. Sure enough, she gave me a fish.

Now something strange happened. Mark got into

the water and put soft rubber cups over my eyes. I could not see and I squealed in protest.

I pulled away from Mark and swam around the pool as fast as I could. I hoped the rush of water would dislodge the cups. When that did not work, I jumped high in the air and crashed into the water on my side. The cup smacked against the water, but it stuck fast to my head. Three times I leaped and crashed. Three times the cup stayed tight against my head.

There seemed nothing I could do to shake the cups loose. I snapped my jaws and shook my head in anger. Then I gave up. Whistling unhappily, I swam to the side of the pool and pressed my forehead against the wall. Mark swam to my side. He stroked me and made soothing sounds.

When I calmed down, he rang the bell, asking me to bring him the ring. This was easy. Under the water I could see with my farsensor. I scanned the bottom with short blasts. The echoes showed me exactly where the ring lay. I carried it to the surface.

Mark and Soooh made loud, happy noises when I stuck my beak out of the water holding the ring. They took off the cups. Mark hugged me, and the sounds he made told me that he was pleased with my work.

What I did wasn't so surprising. Any dolphin can find objects without using her eyes. But to humans, who can't see with sounds, it was a wonderful thing.

Within a few days, the trainers taught Sea Fan and Flasher to find objects while blindfolded. Flasher was so excited at being a part of our work that he was slow to learn. Long after Sea Fan was getting a fish for every dive, he still brought up whatever he first encountered — a stray fish, a large shell, an empty can that had washed in with the tide. When he got no fish, he squeaked with surprise. At last Sea Fan took pity on him and told him to stick to the ring. He made no more mistakes.

It was not long before the humans in white clothes came back. They watched us bring up the ring without using our eyes. They pointed at us and made sounds at one another. When the visiting humans left, Soooh put a tentacle up to her forehead. It seemed to have some kind of meaning because two of the visitors did the same thing. I wondered if they would get a fish for learning the trick so quickly.

The next morning Mark and Soooh herded Sea Fan and Flasher into the performance tank. Before I could follow, Mark gave me the command to fetch the ring. I brought it up and collected my fish. Then I noticed the passage to the performance tank was closed.

At the other end of the enclosure, an opening

appeared in the fence. If I swam quickly into the channel, I could reach the open sea and freedom. Yet I did not move. Snapper was out there, all by himself. I knew that I should go look for him. I could protect him.

As I hovered at the shallow end of the enclosure, I felt bad inside. But I did not want to leave Paradise Cove. If I did, I would never see Mark again.

Mark slipped into the water and swam by me to the gate. He stopped, turned, and called my name. When I understood that I would be with Mark, I joined him. He swam through the opening and down the channel toward the sea.

Side by side we swam the length of the channel. At the end, a broad lagoon lay before us. With two strokes of my tail, I was into the middle of the lagoon. I sped around and around between the pier and land, swimming fast for the first time in months. I whistled for joy as I skimmed through clear water over wrinkled sand.

When I tired of swimming alone, I looked for Mark. He was beside the pier, his head bobbing above the water. I swam over to him and nodded my head toward the water, inviting him to dive. We played dolphin games for a long time.

The sun was high overhead when Soooh came onto the pier. She pulled on a black suit that covered her from neck to feet. Then she climbed down a ladder into a small boat. Mark scrambled over the side and joined her. He put on a suit just like hers.

With a roar, the boat jumped away from the pier. It rushed through the water, leaving a foamy wake.

I was excited. I followed the boat, leaping out of the water with every stroke of my tail. Just outside the lagoon, I passed the boat and turned back. I caught the bow wave and surfed it as we sped along the coast.

After a while, the boat's engine stopped and it glided ahead. Mark hooked a floating buoy and tied up. He pulled on his mask and jumped into the water.

He looked strange. On his back were two metal tanks. A tube ran from the tanks to his mouth. At first I didn't like this new Mark. Then we dove, and I discovered that he could stay underwater longer than I could. He could stay underwater forever — like a fish.

While we were swimming, Mark took a metal ring from his belt and dropped it. This ring was different from the one he had used in the pool. As the ring sank below the surface, a light attached to its side began flashing. Each time the light flashed, there was a click. Mark gave the signal, asking me to bring back the ring.

I rose to the surface, opened my blowhole, and filled my lungs. Then I dove after the ring, which was out of sight. As I swam toward the bottom, I swung my head back and forth, using my farsensor to search the ocean floor. Soon I heard clicks, but they came from the side. The current had carried the ring away from the spot where Mark waited on the surface.

I swam past several bass and over a sole that lay half buried in the sand. I reached the ring, poked my beak through it, and carried it to the surface. That dive changed our lives.

17

On the morning that I left Paradise Cove there was a bright sun and a brisk breeze. I left on a boat. I lay on a foam pad that rested on a canvas sling. Above stretched a cloth to protect me from the burning sun. Mark poured seawater over my sides to keep me cool.

I did not like being in the air. I felt heavy and hot. Mark could see that I was upset. He talked to me and stroked my back and belly. That made me feel better.

The boat roared through the water, faster than a dolphin could swim. It roared across the sea until the sun was high overhead.

At last the motor stopped and the boat began to pitch in the swells. It was a funny feeling. Mark made soothing sounds. I think he was telling me that we had reached the end of our journey.

Humans grabbed the sling and lifted it over the side of the boat. It tilted, and I slid into the sea. The cool water closed over my head and I wriggled with joy.

I was in a large pen. Netting hung down from a

floating frame anchored in water as deep as ten dolphins, stacked flukes to beak. The frame was a flipper length above the water. It was flat and wide enough for humans to walk on. In one corner of the pen, about half a dolphin length beneath the surface, was a wooden platform.

When I leaped, I could see that my pen was anchored in the open sea. On the distant shore, where waves broke upon the sand, a pier stretched into the water. Land caves clustered behind it. This was a place I had never seen before.

My new home was lonely. For the first few days I was left to myself. Each morning, Soooh came in a small boat, bringing my dinner. She fed me all the smelt and mackerel I could eat. She made pleasant sounds and stroked me, but left when the fish was gone. I was glad to see her, but I wanted Mark. I wondered why he did not come.

I spent my days playing with kelp that floated by and small fish that swam in through the netting. I watched cormorants drop into the sea with a splash and a shower of spray, then bob to the surface with wriggling fish. Gulls screamed. Pelicans, tired of skimming over the water, perched on my pen to sleep. Often I picked up echoes of large fish far away, and twice I detected sea lions.

Once a sea elephant swam close. He was much bigger than me but not as big as an orca. He floated at the surface with his head out of the water. I whistled my name. He looked at me but did not answer. Then he snorted. He swung his head, shaking the hump that hung over his mouth so that it flopped back and forth. I called again, but he lost interest and swam away.

After seven suns, Mark came back. I jumped and whistled with excitement. My heart beat fast. I had never been so happy to see another being — even another dolphin.

For a long time, Mark stood on the underwater platform and stroked my side. He gave me several fine fish. Then he opened the gate and swam into the open sea. He called, and I followed him.

Mark climbed back into his boat. He started south, and I went with him, surfing the bow wave. We traveled along the coast until we reached another boat.

When we arrived, two divers went over the side of the other boat. They sank fast and soon were out of sight. Mark slipped into the water and swam to the spot where the divers had disappeared. I followed.

From far below came a familiar click, click, click. I looked at Mark. He signaled, and I dove toward the sounds. As I got closer, I could see the flashing light. Its rays cut through the dark water.

With an extra burst of speed, I reached the light,

which was in a diver's hand. I peered into the faceplate and saw that the diver was Soooh. She gave me a fish and turned off her light. The bright colors faded and the world grew dim.

Then I heard another train of clicks in back of me. I swam toward the sound and found another clicking light in the hand of the other diver. This diver was a stranger, but he had a bag of fish just like Soooh's.

When we came to the surface later, I discovered that the humans called the new diver "Rick." Rick had black hair, like Mark's, but when he took off his mask, his hair bristled like the spines of a sea urchin.

As the divers clicked their lights on and off, I swam back and forth between them. Soon each diver was surrounded by a silver cloud of small fish, drawn by the flashing lights and the bits of fish that fell into the water.

The game was so much fun that I ignored the little fish. I ignored them even though the water was so crowded that the divers had trouble feeding me. I didn't even think of eating the little fish until the game was finished.

Each time I came to the surface for air, Mark made happy sounds and stroked me. After the divers came back to their boats, Mark and I swam together before we returned to my pen.

We played the light game with the divers for several

days. Each day we dived deeper, and each day the divers were farther apart.

I learned to listen for a special signal from a diver, then pick up a line from Mark and carry it far through the dark to where the diver waited. From the humans' actions and my small store of human sounds, I decided that I was learning to rescue a diver in trouble. It was all for something that the humans called the "navy," whatever that was.

In the afternoons, Mark and I played together like a pair of dolphins. When we got tired, we swam side by side, with my flipper resting on his shoulder. I was happy. I forgot my pod back at Paradise Cove. I forgot about Snapper. I forgot about my family in Glacier Strait.

Before dawn one morning, a north wind sprang up. Clouds covered the sky, and rain fell steadily on the gray sea. White foam covered the thrusting swells that became great waves. The wind tore off their tops and sent mists of spray sailing through the air.

I was left alone. I stayed near the bottom of my pen, where the water was not as rough. When I came up to breathe, the rain stung my skin.

Toward dusk, I saw a small boat start from shore. It moved carefully through the surf, dodging the breaking waves. I could see the boat rise high on the crest of a wave, then sink into the trough that separated it from the next wave. Twice the boat made its way safely over a wave. Then the largest wave of all crashed down on the boat.

The boat vanished from sight. I watched. Two heads bobbed to the surface. The humans stood up in the shallow water and pushed the boat back to shore. They could not come through the rough sea.

There was no food that day. All I had to eat were a few small fish that wandered into my pen.

The next day was the same. I was alone in driving wind and slashing rain. My pen rose and fell with each wave. Big branches of kelp, torn loose by the surging water, caught on the posts and trailed across the frame.

I thought about leaving. Weighed down by kelp, one corner of the pen was almost under water. It would be easy to leap out and swim away. But then I would never see Mark again. Hungry as I was, I waited.

18

On the third morning, the rain drifted off. The wind howled as hard as ever. It drove the sea into heaving swells. There was no way for a boat to reach my pen. My hunger grew until it was as big as the waves that surged toward shore.

I was tail-walking so that I could watch the shore when I heard a strange sound. The sound did not come from a boat. It did not come from any sea creature. The sound came from the sky.

Frightened, I dove to the bottom of the pen. The noise grew louder and louder. I stared up at the shining white surface, expecting to see a monster. I saw nothing. The noise became so loud that it filled the world. I huddled in the corner and waited.

Suddenly, there was a splash. Something silvery blue sank toward me. It was a mackerel. I snatched it up. It tasted wonderful. Another splash. Another mackerel.

Somehow Mark had managed to bring me food. I swam up and burst into the air.

Directly overhead was a big metal bird. The horrible noise came from this bird. It hovered above the pen without moving. Its turning blades made a wind that flattened the water below and sent waves in every direction.

From a large opening in the bird's side, a fish dropped. It splashed into the water outside my pen, where I couldn't reach it.

I squealed with distress. When the next fish dropped, I leaped into the air and caught it. As I swallowed it, I saw Mark looking down at me.

I whistled with delight. With small, steady movements of my flippers, I stayed half out of the water. I kept my eye on the metal bird and my mouth open.

Mark leaned far out over the water. A line around his middle kept him from falling into the sea. He drew back his arm and threw. A fish landed in my open mouth. Mark threw fish until my stomach was full.

When the fish were gone, the metal bird rose high in the air and flew off toward the shore. The noise of the whirling blades faded in the distance.

With my hunger gone, I thought of other things besides food. Mainly, I wondered how Silver was and what the rest of the pod was doing. It was the first time I had thought about the pod since I left Paradise Cove. But I didn't think about them very long. Instead, I thought about Mark and how he had flown through the air to bring me food. I felt warm inside.

I dreamed about swimming with Mark in water clear as air. Rays of sunlight turned the green water golden. Tiny red and yellow and silver fishes swam around us. Then a sharp whistle drove the picture from my head.

The sound was familiar. I had heard it many times before. I could hardly believe my bones.

Again the sound cut through the water: "Silver! Silver!"

"Coral! Coral!" I whistled. I scanned the water with my farsensor and detected Silver moving fast. He drew close and called again.

I answered him.

At last he burst into the air beside my pen. He spun twice, then tail-walked. With a wild whistle, he leaped over the barrier and joined me in the pen.

This was not the Silver I had left sulking in the corner of his solitary pool. His whistle was clear and happy.

I sent the signal that meant a question. I wanted to know how Silver had left Paradise Cove.

"Storm," Silver whistled. He sent pictures of the tide running high and the wind piling the water even higher. The water level in his enclosure rose, and he jumped over the fence and swam to the sea.

Again I sent the question signal, followed by "Sea

Fan. Flasher." I wanted to know about the rest of the pod.

Silver signaled "No. No." He sent pictures of him jumping over the fence twice to show Sea Fan and Flasher how easy it was. He begged them to leave with him, but they refused. They liked it in Paradise Cove.

"Silver. Silver." I signaled, telling him that he once liked it there, too.

"No more," he replied. He sent pictures of Spray's lifeless body and himself swimming alone. For a moment he sounded sad.

I reminded him how much he had liked playing with the humans and performing in the shows.

He sent back pictures of himself in a tiny pool where the walls sent the click trains back into his skull like shark's teeth. Where he could not swim fast or far. Where he never saw any new creatures. Where he could never explore new parts of the sea. He explained that, with Spray at his side, he didn't miss these things. But now she was gone.

The sadness came back. Silver smacked the water with his tail. "White Fang, yes," he whistled. He told me that Paradise Cove was no life for an orca and that it was no life for a dolphin.

I bubbled in protest. "Coral. Fine," I whistled. I pictured myself leaving the pen every day and swimming with Mark in the open sea. I showed us playing wonderful games in the deeps.

Silver snorted, making loud pops with his blowhole. "Coral not fine," he whistled. His sound pictures told a strange story. They showed Mark growing flippers and dorsal fin and flukes like a dolphin. Silver believed that I confused Mark with a dolphin. He pictured me waiting at the edge of the enclosure for Mark to appear. Then he pictured Mark at the edge of the water and my heart beating as if I'd been racing a shark.

Silver's pictures upset me. They bewildered me. I rolled away from my brother and dove down, down to the bottom of the pen. I wanted to think. I knew that Mark was a human and I was a dolphin. What Silver thought was silly, and there was no truth in it. At least that's what I kept telling myself.

19

At the first streaks of dawn, Silver jumped into the open sea. He swam out of sight but never out of sensor range.

When Mark and I traveled south to join the divers, Silver followed. He stayed about ten boat lengths behind us, swimming far to one side.

Silver moved close and watched me work. He hovered in silence, exhaling underwater so there was no misty cloud to reveal his presence. When he wanted to breathe, he barely broke the surface with his blowhole. None of the humans noticed their silent companion.

I was moving deep into the sea, on my way to take the rescue line to Soooh, when Silver whistled softly.

"Let's surprise them," he said.

He cut in front of me, stuck his beak through the ring, and swam off with the line. He delivered the line to Soooh, moving so swiftly that she did not realize she was working with a different dolphin. Together, we swam to the surface.

When we burst into the air, Mark shouted with surprise. He recognized Silver at once.

"It's Romeo!" he said. He tossed each of us a fish, then made happy sounds. He was pleased to see my brother.

Silver and I took turns carrying the line to the divers. We worked until the sun was high overhead.

After the divers climbed into their boat and left, Mark and I frolicked in the water. Several times Mark invited Silver to join our game, but my brother kept his distance. When we started back, Silver swam off toward the open sea.

A few nights later Silver came to my pen. He swam rapidly, leaping into the air to speed his journey. He was excited about something.

"What? What?" I signaled.

"Sea Fan! Sea Fan!" he answered. He told me that he had met Sea Fan in the open sea. She was working with new divers from the navy. Flasher was back at Paradise Cove working alone on a dreadful task. His job was to ram dead sharks as they were pulled through the water.

I whistled angrily at the thought of Flasher spending his days in a tank with sharks — even though they were not alive.

Only a human could think up a project so terrible. A shark's skin is so rough that it feels like a million sharp teeth ripping at your beak. Dolphins sometimes ram sharks, but only to save another dolphin's life.

I pictured Flasher's beak and forehead covered with cuts and bruises.

"No," Silver whistled. He pictured Flasher with a soft rubber pad covering his beak.

"Why?" I whistled. I could not understand why humans would make the little dolphin do something so awful.

Silver told me that Sea Fan thought Flasher was learning to protect divers from shark attacks.

I snorted with disgust. "Nothing to learn," I signaled. Any dolphin would ram a shark that attacked a diver. Nobody had to teach us how.

Silver agreed. He sent his favorite signal — "Stupid," followed by "humans," many times. He pictured Flasher's trainer and whistled "navy." He looked at me for a long time. Whistling "navy" again, he pictured Soooh teaching me to play games with sharks.

I told Silver that I thought we were practicing the rescue of divers.

He fell silent. After a time he pictured a human gasping for breath and signaled, "Need you. Need you." He reminded me that humans were not meant to stay underwater. "Swim slow," he whistled. "Breathe often." He pictured them carrying air tanks on their backs whenever they went into the dark water. Then he told me something I did not know. When humans came up too fast from the deeps, they got sick or died.

I didn't answer. I knew Silver was trying to tell me that Mark could not live in the sea. He wanted me to think more about dolphins and less about Mark.

To block out the unwanted sounds, I sprayed the sea with sensor clicks. The echoes from a school of sardines drowned Silver's signals.

My brother knew what I was doing. Rising half out of the water, he nodded his head and clapped his jaws. His eye gleamed with the cold light of stars. He told me once again that Mark was not a dolphin.

With a slap of his tail, he leaped out of the pen and swam off. Soon he was so far away that my sensor could not detect him. I was alone.

The next morning white puffy clouds floated in a blue sky. A gentle wind blew toward land. Mark came to the pen in a new boat. This one had an opening in the side almost down to the waterline. Mark taught me to leap out of the water and onto a soft pad in the bottom of the boat.

After I slid onto the pad several times, we started south. This time I rode in the boat beside Mark. We traveled much farther from land than we usually worked.

At the place where we stopped, a large yellow platform floated in the sea. Tied to the far end of the platform was a boat much larger than ours. On the platform, several humans were bending over strange objects. Mark tied up our boat and made the loud noises that humans use to call one another. The humans made similar noises and pointed toward the sea where a steady stream of bubbles broke the surface. Something was blowing out air from below.

Mark signaled and I slid backward into the sea. As my head sank under the water, I heard the click, click, click of a diver's signal. Down into the water I dove. At first the sea was clear as air. I sank into the deep blue depths. The light faded. I could see only a short way, but that made no difference to me.

I swam deeper than we had ever gone before. At last I reached the diver. Soooh hovered near a large object bigger than the bird that carried Mark to my pen. Metal pipes at each corner held it a dolphin's length above the ocean floor. It was hollow. Echoes told me that inside it were other humans. I was looking at a human cave on the bottom of the sea.

When I touched Soooh's mask with my beak, she did not give me a fish as she usually did. That puzzled me, but I was not hungry. I stood on my tail and waited.

Soooh swam over to the side of the cave. She put one tentacle on a round reel attached to the side of the cave. A long line, like the one I had been carrying back and forth between divers, was wound on the reel.

At its tip was a metal ring. She bent her head in the direction of the reel.

I knew what to do. I stuck my beak inside the ring and scanned the ocean in all directions. From a distance, I picked up the clicks of another diver.

With strong strokes of my tail, I swam rapidly to Rick. He took the ring, but did not give me a fish either.

The rules of the game were changing, but I could not wait around to find out. I was almost out of breath. I shot to the surface and sucked air through my blowhole.

Mark was waiting for me. He gave me two fat fish. I understood the new rules. From now on, I had to finish the job before I was fed.

Our work went so well that Mark started a new game. He gave me another ring like the one on the rescue line. This ring was not connected to a line. Instead, a metal box dangled from it.

I stuck my beak through the ring and got another fish. After a while, Mark would not feed me unless I swam away with the box. Then he refused to give me a fish even though I swam four boat lengths toward shore.

I swam back and glided in front of Mark, looking closely at him. He raised an arm and dropped it toward the water.

Suddenly, I understood. I carried the ring down to the bottom and let Soooh take it from me. She opened the box and took out a metal tool. Then she put something in the box, closed it, and held up the ring so I could slip my beak through it. I carried the box back to Mark and got my fish.

It wasn't long before I figured out the new game. It wasn't much different from Rescue the Diver. I was carrying tools back and forth from the surface. I supposed I could take signals back and forth as well.

When we finished the day's work, Soooh and Rick did not go to the surface. Instead, they swam over to the cave and dived beneath it. They disappeared, but I could sense them inside. The undersea cave seemed to be their home.

I wondered if the cave had always been there and they just happened to find it. Hermit crabs lived in discarded shells they found on the ocean floor. I saw no reason why humans couldn't do the same thing.

All afternoon an image of the strange cave stayed in my head. The image stayed clear even while Mark and I played our usual games. Maybe humans were learning to stay in the water. It was a startling notion. As I swam back and forth across Mark's legs, I thought how nice it would be if he lived in the sea.

20

~~~~~~~~~~~~~~~~~~~~~~~~~~~~~~~~~~~~~~

While we worked with Soooh and Rick on the ocean floor, the moon dwindled to a thin white line and grew big again. Some days Silver joined us, but always he swam away as soon as the divers went into their undersea home. He wanted no part of the games with Mark.

For some reason, the work with the divers stopped. There wasn't much for me to do. I became so bored that I teased bass that swam through the netting. As a fish glided by, I grabbed it and held it lightly in my jaws. Its tail stuck out on one side of my beak and the head on the other. The bass always struggled. When it got very angry, I stopped swimming. Slowly I opened my mouth and waited. The bass seemed startled. Then it swam away. Just before the bass reached the netting, I grabbed it again. I usually did this several times. Then I let it go. I was never hungry, and, besides, kelp bass was not my favorite food.

I spent most of my time swimming and dreaming. I was waiting for Mark. Every day he came to visit me. After he fed me, we swam together inside the pen. It wasn't as much fun as romping in the open sea, but I was content.

One day as I was drifting, half asleep, a torrent of whistles burst through the water. It was a herd of dolphins, whistling their name signals. Sensor echoes showed a herd of bottlenose dolphins approaching from the north. There were almost as many of them as there are suns from one full moon to the next. If they stayed on course, they would pass my pen on the seaward side, a good many dolphin lengths from me.

"Coral! Coral!" I whistled.

The dolphins whistled back and veered in my direction. Before long, there were gray dolphins leaping all around me. Bottlenose dolphins are half again as long as white-sided dolphins, and their mouths curve up at each side, making them look like happy humans.

The dolphins showered me with question whistles. They wanted to know what I was doing in the pen.

I told them that I worked with human divers and that I lived in the pen.

They thought I was foolish to stay in a tiny square of ocean when I could leap over the side at any time and swim free.

It was hard for me to explain that I liked working with humans. I put pictures in their heads of my swims with Mark, but they were not impressed.

Because they had come from the north, I wondered if they had seen my little brother. "Snapper?" I signaled. "Snapper? Like me."

Pictures from everywhere crowded into my head, confusing me. The biggest dolphin, a male with a jagged dorsal fin and a pink belly, silenced the rest with a blast of sound. He told me that a young white-sided dolphin had followed them for several weeks. The young dolphin, whose name signal was "Snapper," stayed close for protection and shared in their fishing. One day when they were moving toward the open sea, they met an enormous herd of white-sided dolphins. The young dolphin became excited at meeting so many dolphins like himself and left to swim with the new herd.

I was glad that Snapper was safe, but I wondered if I would ever see my little brother again.

The dolphins signaled that it was time to leave. As they turned to go, the big, pink-bellied male invited me to join their herd.

Without hesitating, I refused.

When Mark came with my food that afternoon, Soooh was in the boat. She helped feed me, and when Mark slipped into the water to play, she joined us.

Soooh could swim almost as well as Mark, and she seemed to like our games. But I wished she were back on the bottom of the sea. When Soooh came, Mark still petted me, but not as often. Sometimes, instead of swimming with me, Mark and Soooh swam together. I didn't like that much.

As the days passed, things got worse. When Mark and I swam together, Soooh stayed at Mark's side. Mark didn't mind. He wanted the three of us to play together. But I minded.

I wondered how I could get rid of Soooh. Then I remembered some of the tricks we learned at Paradise Cove. I offered Mark my dorsal fin. He grasped it. I towed him as far away from Soooh as I could get without leaping out of the pen.

We swam around the pen. Soooh watched us, but did not try to join us. I whistled happily. Mark stroked the top of my head. But when the ride ended, Mark swam to Soooh.

"Nicki," he called. He bobbed his head toward the water, inviting me to join them.

I stayed on my side of the pen. I didn't want to swim with Soooh. I sank to the bottom and rested on the netting. I stayed down for a long time. When I ran out of air, I came up, filled my lungs, and went back down. Finally, Mark and Soooh got back into the boat and left.

When they were gone, I swam slowly about the pen. I didn't feel like jumping or diving or tail-walking. I ignored the small fish that swam around me. For the first time, I felt lonely.

I wished I were back in Glacier Strait, fishing for anchovies and young salmon. I wanted to play games with my friends. I wondered if White Fang's orcas had left the strait and whether I had a new sister or brother. I thought of Mother with a new baby and remembered how she used to stroke my side. The thought made me sad.

After the sun sank into the sea, Silver came swimming through the night. He leaped into my pen and splashed me. When he gave a play signal, I pretended I didn't see it.

"Wrong? Wrong?" he signaled. He pictured me frolicking in the water and whistled the question "Where happy Coral?" He wanted to know why I seemed so sad.

I didn't answer.

He told me that new divers were living in the undersea cave. Sea Fan worked with them every day, learning to rescue divers and carry boxes.

I still didn't answer.

Silver sang a funny song about the divers in their black suits and bubbling tanks. He pretended to be a diver. He bounced along the bottom of the tank like a diver waiting on the ocean floor for a dolphin. He stood on his head like a diver inspecting something on the bottom. He burst into the air and threw his head back like a diver who wanted to clear water from a mask. He was so funny that I snorted with pleasure.

"Good," Silver whistled.

I told him I was sad and signaled that I wanted to go home.

Silver whistled rapidly, with the question signal following each sound "Home?" he asked. "Home? Yes? Yes?"

I thought about the long swim back. I almost said "Yes." Then I thought about Mark. I couldn't leave him. "No," I whistled, so softly that Silver could barely hear me.

The next few days Mark came alone. I was happy again and almost forgot about Soooh. I forgot about her until the day Mark brought her to the pen again.

This time things went wrong. We finished a game of Keep the Kelp. Soooh was on the far side of the pen, treading water. Mark was stroking my side and making pleasant sounds.

Soooh waved, and Mark swam over to her. He laid his tentacle across her shoulder and made the sound humans use to signal happiness. I got angry. I had bad thoughts about Soooh.

I swam beneath her and grabbed her plastic fin in

my teeth. I shook it hard. It came halfway off her fluke.

Soooh laughed. She thought I was playing. She straightened the fin and swam to the center of the pen.

I swam over and grabbed the heavy rope of hair that trailed behind her. I jerked it hard.

She put a tentacle to her head and whirled around to face me. Her laughter stopped. Her eyes were as round as sand dollars.

I decided to teach Soooh a lesson. I tugged at her mask. It slipped to one side. Water flooded in and covered her blowhole.

Soooh kicked to the surface. She tilted back her head and pulled the bottom of the mask away from her face. The water drained out. She adjusted the strap at the back of her head. She gave me a strange look. I could taste fear seeping through the water.

I reared up out of the water and whacked her on the head with my beak, but not very hard. Again her mask dislodged. The taste of fear grew strong, but Soooh stayed in the water.

I lowered my head and bumped her.

Soooh made frightened sounds.

Mark swam to her side. Soft sounds came from his blowhole. He held Soooh around her middle and made more sounds. She shook her head.

Mark looked at me. Still holding Soooh, he made hard, unhappy sounds. He was scolding me. He had never done that before.

I swam into the corner of the pen. I wondered why Mark was so angry. I didn't hurt Soooh, but I could easily have done so. I could have ripped off her mask and sent it dropping to the ocean floor. I could have held her underwater until she drowned. I just wanted her to leave.

No one seemed to have fun after that. In a little while, Mark and Soooh climbed back into the boat and returned to shore. I was not sorry to see them go.

21

From the day I frightened Soooh, Mark came to the pen by himself. I thought that would make me happy, but it didn't. We still played Keep the Kelp and Stand on Your Head and Hide-and-Seek. Mark still stroked me each day. But he didn't stay as long as he used to. When we swam side by side, he often seemed to be thinking about something else.

After a time, we began diving at the undersea cave again. Soooh worked with me, but she no longer trusted me. When I carried something to her, she kept her eyes on me. Her muscles were tight, and she was ready to flee.

One day the wind blew warm from the south, and the sea was calm and clear. The work went so well that no one wanted to stop. We worked far into the afternoon, long past the time when the divers usually went back into their undersea cave.

On my final trip, I followed the clicking light and found Soooh crumpled on the sand. She lay still. Only her rope of hair moved, swaying in the current like a strand of kelp.

I swam over and nudged her with my beak. Soooh was limp. I nudged her harder, and she flopped onto her back. As she turned, her breathing tube dropped from her blowhole and dangled from her chest. Her eyes were closed. I whistled. They did not open.

Soooh needed air. I thought about carrying her to the surface. It might have worked, but Silver's warning flashed through my head. The fast trip from the deeps was dangerous for humans. I tried to think.

I swam toward the rescue reel, but came back. The humans did not know she was in trouble, and she could not hang onto the ring.

Perhaps I could get Soooh into the humans' cave. I had seen divers swim in and out and knew that the entrance was on the bottom.

I looked from the cave to Soooh. She lay about a dolphin length away, beside some big tanks that were fastened to the metal frame. The tanks hid her from any human who looked through the viewing port.

I worked my beak beneath her body and pushed hard. The weights on Soooh's belt made her heavy, but she rose slightly off the ocean floor.

I slipped under her and shoved again. Soooh's body moved a flipper length. With a few shoves, I had her on the sand beneath the cave. It seemed as if I had been shoving her forever, but it took only seconds.

I rolled on my side and looked up. Just above us was a large hole in the metal skin. The water in the hole gleamed silver. That meant we were close to air.

I wiggled under Soooh's body. I tensed my muscles and heaved with all my strength. Soooh burst through the opening. I stuck my head into the air and saw her lying sprawled on the floor. I squealed for help.

Nothing happened. I squealed again.

A nearby wall opened, and a human stepped through. The human dropped to its knees and ripped Soooh's mask off her face. The human put its head beside Soooh's blowhole and listened. Then it pressed its own blowhole against hers and puffed air into her lungs. After the human did this several times, Soooh's eyes fluttered open. Her chest moved up and down as she gulped air.

I turned back into the sea and swam to the surface. I felt happy. Soooh was alive.

The day after Soooh's accident there was no diving. When Mark came to the pen, he put his arms around me and told me how glad he was that I helped Soooh. He said her name many times, but I didn't listen. I lay quietly, with my eyes shut, enjoying the caresses.

After I ate, Mark took me out of the pen. For a long time we played together in the open sea. I had so much fun that I didn't want him to leave. If Mark lived in the cave beneath the sea, he would never have to go back on land.

The more I thought about it, the better I liked the idea. I would capture Mark for myself, and he would always be with me. We could swim all day.

With a burst of joy, I dove deep and silently glided up behind him. Gently, so gently he did not feel it, I pulled on one fin, then on the other. Mark turned in a slow circle, and his legs spread wide apart.

When I surfaced beneath him, I lifted him out of the water. He was perched between my blowhole and my dorsal fin, with one leg hanging down on each side.

I began to swim in the direction of the undersea cave. With no current to help us, I would have to carry him for more than an hour into the open ocean. I knew I could do it.

At first, Mark made happy sounds. He stroked my head. He sang to me, pitching his deep human voice as high as he could. He whistled like a dolphin.

Scattered puffs of clouds drifted across the sky. A breeze stirred the sea, making tiny waves. I stroked steadily, driving my flukes deep into the water. Behind us trailed a wake of glittering foam. My heart was filled with bliss.

After a while Mark looked back. His songs stopped.

He fell silent. The only sound was the rushing of our bodies through the water. As Mark realized how far we were from the boat, I felt his legs tighten against my sides.

He leaned forward. "Nicki! Nicki!" he said. "Back. Back."

I understood, but I kept swimming. I swam even faster.

We were halfway to the place where the cave rested on the ocean floor. Mark's boat was now so far away that he could not reach it without my help.

The wind picked up. I was swimming against swells that deepened as the wind grew strong. With Mark on my back, I had to stay on the surface. The cresting waves grew higher and higher. Each time we hit one, the spray slapped Mark in the face. He coughed and turned his head. It was hard for him to breathe.

Mark was frightened. He pressed his knee into my side, telling me to turn back.

I kept swimming toward the setting sun, trying not to hear Mark's gasps for air. We would soon reach the cave, I told myself. Then I would take Mark into the depths to his new home. We would be happy together.

As I pictured our dive to the bottom of the sea, my joy faded. Mark's back was bare. He never used air tanks when we swam together. I had forgotten that humans had to take along their air when they went deep into the sea. Mark would drown before we reached the cave.

With a whistle of despair, I turned abruptly back toward shore. Each shoreward stroke of my flukes put my dream farther out of reach. As we came alongside the boat, the sun slipped below the horizon, taking my hopes with it. With a heavy heart, I watched Mark climb aboard and leave for land.

22

Late that night when I was drifting sadly around my pen, there was a great splash. I looked up and found Silver beside me.

I didn't want to face what had happened that afternoon, and so I just told him that there had been no diving lately.

Silver was not surprised. He already knew about Soooh's accident and filled my head with pictures of her lying on the ocean floor.

I asked how he found out.

Silver told me that he had heard the navy divers on Sea Fan's boat. He still didn't know how the accident had happened because humans talked so slowly that he could not understand all their signals.

The pictures I put in his head showed everything. First, Soooh running out of air and lying on the sand, then me swimming up and shoving her into the undersea cave and whistling for help. I even showed a human making her breathe again.

Silver wanted to know why I had bothered to save a stupid human, especially one I didn't like. He thought I should have swum away and let the humans take care of one another. He reminded me about all the whales and dolphins and seals and otter that had been killed by humans.

I gave Silver a funny look. I hadn't thought about those other humans for a long time. Mostly, I was too busy working or playing with Mark or thinking about him to think about anybody else. I thought about them now. Humans were not all alike, just as dolphins were not all alike. Some were evil, some were kind, and some didn't seem to know what they were doing.

I thought about Soooh, too. When I thought about the way she swam with Mark, I still got angry. But that was no reason to let her die.

I bobbed my head and whistled sharply. "Glad," I signaled. "Coral glad." I told Silver that Soooh was not like the humans who killed sea creatures, and I did not want to be like them either.

Silver's blowhole spluttered. This was a new idea to him. He took several breaths before he signaled, "Soooh no dolphin killer. Coral right."

Silver's approval gave me courage. I took a big breath, then signaled that he would not be pleased when he found out what I had done with Mark.

"What?" he asked.

I pictured Mark staying with me in the sea and whistled, "Want. Want." Then I showed him all that had happened that afternoon, how I had taken Mark away from his boat and carried him out to the under-sea cave. I was not proud when I showed him that Mark almost drowned before I brought him back.

Silver asked how I felt about what I had done.

I felt ashamed. I had been thinking a lot about Mark's brush with death. I knew that humans who lived in the cave always carried air tanks when they came into the water. I knew that they had to stay in the deeps while they lived beneath the sea. I knew that if Mark lived in the cave, he could never play and leap with me at the surface. I knew my plan had been foolish. And I knew I had almost killed Mark. It was hard to speak.

I whistled softly. "Feel bad," I signaled.

There was sadness in Silver's eye. He stretched out a flipper and gently stroked my side.

We lay together quietly in the black water. The night was dark, and there was no moon. After a time, Silver sang of home. It was a song he had sung many times, but I had not heard him sing it since the day he left Glacier Strait. As I listened, my sadness lifted, but only a little.

The song ended. The whistles trailed away into the night.

Silver turned his eye on me. He told me that he had news for me.

I waited, expecting to hear something about the humans.

Instead he pictured Flasher swimming in the open sea. "Free," he signaled. "Free."

I whistled the signal for question.

Silver described Flasher's last day with the humans. He told me that the navy divers had put Flasher in a boat and taken him from Paradise Cove into the open sea. They wanted him to practice ramming sharks. As soon as the boat stopped and the humans slid Flasher into the water, he fled.

"When?" I asked.

Silver pictured the sun rising and setting three times.

"Where? Where? Flasher? Where?" I asked why Flasher had not come to my pen.

Silver laughed so hard that his bubbles made the sea foam. He told me that Flasher would never go anyplace where he might meet a diver. He wanted no part of any game that involved sharks. For the past two days, Flasher had been in a shallow bay just a few leagues up the coast.

"Sea Fan?" I asked.

Silver's whistle lost its happy lilt. "Afraid," he signaled. He told me that Sea Fan felt safe diving with the navy, but feared life in the open sea. Unless she encountered a herd of spinners, she would never leave.

The sky above the shore grew light, and Silver got ready to leave. He stood on his tail and, turning his head to one side, gazed down at me.

"I'm off," he whistled.

"Where?" I asked.

He didn't answer for a long time. There was a faraway look in his eye. When he replied, my head filled with pictures of the western seas, where the sun set each night. I saw warm waters filled with strange and wonderful creatures.

I tried to change his mind. I filled his head with pictures of Glacier Strait and the home pod.

Silver whistled with disbelief when I suggested he go home. He told me he could not go back to Glacier Strait. He was too old to rejoin Mother's pod, and he was too young to become leader of the herd. He would never be happy taking orders again.

I reminded Silver that Father wanted him to come home and help protect the herd.

Silver clapped his beak. With a toss of his head, he informed me that the pod was no longer in danger. By now, White Fang had reached northern waters. If the biggest orca stopped eating dolphins, so would the rest of his pod. Then Silver asked me why I stayed in a pen I could leave at any time. He waited for me to say something.

He was right, just as the bottlenose dolphins had been right. Nothing stopped me from leaping into the sea. The sides of my pen were so low that even a baby dolphin could clear them.

Pictures filled my head. Pictures of Mark. Pictures of Flasher. Pictures of Snapper. Pictures of home. I did not answer Silver. I wasn't sure what I wanted to say.

The sun came up in a blaze of fire. I rose high in the water and stared at the shore, but the sun blinded me and I could see nothing.

I dove to the bottom of my pen, then rose slowly, listening to the sounds of the sea. Fish squeaked and grunted. Crabs popped like bubbles bursting. In the distance, I heard the deep moan of a whale. I picked up echoes from a bat ray as it swept silently through the water, its wings extended. The ray was searching for unwary clams. When it found one, it scooped the clam from the sand and crushed the shell with its broad, flat teeth.

I had been away for a long time. By now the young salmon were moving down the streams into the strait. The gray whales were on their way north with their calves. As I thought, my secret heart became clear.

My wishes lay uncovered as a wave uncovers a shell hidden in the sand. I knew what I wanted to do.

Rising half out of the water, I faced Silver. I told him that, no matter what he did, I was heading north. After I picked up Flasher, we would search for Snapper. Then we would go to Glacier Strait.

With a surge of determination, I leaped over the platform and into the freedom of my watery world. I did not look back to see if Silver would follow. Turning north, I swam toward home.